Camera Shy

Julia Bogson

Camera Shy

A Novel

Julia Boggio

HOME BY MIDNIGHT PUBLISHING

To request permissions, contact the publisher at hbmpublishingUK@gmail.com.

Paperback: 978-1-7392151-5-6

First edition.

Cover design: Bailey McGinn

A CIP record for this book is available from the British Library.

For Damian,
for being a 'good, one-legged, old
but handsome and wise character'
and to Lesley, for putting up with him

'DID YOU KNOW I WAS S'POSED TO GET ENGAGED TOMORROW NIGHT? Ha!' slurred the blonde English woman. She was sitting alone in the empty bistro, gulping red wine at an alarming pace.

Gabriel, the only other customer, watched from his usual spot in the opposite corner of the outdoor patio. *Somebody* was going to have a nasty hangover in the morning. He swirled his amber cognac, served appropriately in a balloon snifter, as he reflected on how the British drank like heathens.

Aside from the woman's outbursts, the only other sound was the repetitive scraping of a broom against the pavement. Michel, the skinny, buck-toothed waiter, was sweeping up that evening's rubbish. He had been on the receiving end of the woman's monologue for quite a while now. Catching Gabriel's eye, Michel gave him a desperate look that said, *'My mistress is waiting for me. When is this anglaise going to leave?'* As a regular diner, Gabriel had heard plenty over the years about Michel's post-shift antics. The man had questionable morals, but the *steak frites* were good and the bistro was close to Gabriel's apartment building.

He offered a noncommittal shrug in response. Michel rolled his eyes and continued sweeping. Returning to his book, Gabriel re-read the paragraph he had marked with his index finger.

'Two years, down the drain!' she exclaimed, jolting him off the page again. At this rate, he'd never finish this chapter on restoring rotting woodwork.

She seemed determined to draw attention, so he decided to give it to her momentarily. The woman was obviously in pain—he empathised with that. Even though she was fall-down drunk and slumped at her table with streaks of mascara running down her face, Gabriel recognised beauty when he saw it. Her tanned skin glowed with natural, outdoorsy health. Despite all the wine, her perfectly straight teeth dazzled in their whiteness—a poster child for proper dental care in defiance of Britain's reputation for horrible teeth. Long blonde ringlets fell to halfway down her back, reminding him of the woman in the shell in Botticelli's *Birth of Venus*. Unlike Venus, this woman was clothed in a blue, off-the-shoulder summer dress printed with small white flowers. Pity…his photographer's eye imagined she'd look great posing nude in a shell.

As he studied her, she accidentally spilled her wine on the white tablecloth, the red tentacles extending like blood. He stared as it drip, drip, dripped onto the patio floor. Gabriel shivered.

'You!'

It took him a moment to realise she was speaking to him. He pointed to himself.

'Yes, you! You're a man, right?'

'Last time I checked,' Gabriel said in his flawless American-English accent.

'Why are men such wankers?'

Gabriel frowned and glanced at Michel, who definitely fit that description. 'Not all of us are…*wankers*, as you say.'

'What about you? Are you a wanker?'

2

He imagined a few people might think so. 'I suppose it would depend on who you ask. Everybody is a wanker to somebody.'

She nodded as though he were Jean-Paul Sartre, and he had just defined existentialism for the first time. 'Wow! Huh. That's *so true*. Well, Krish is a wanker to me! I thought he was one of the good ones, you know? But then—poof—he tells me he's in love with his ex-girl-friend. And just like that, it's all over.'

Whoever this man was, he must be an idiot.

'*Garçon*! Another bottle *see-voo-play*!' She waved at Michel like drunken royalty. Her French was truly terrible.

Michel leaned on his broom and slapped on his practiced Sympathetic Waiter face. Clicking his tongue three times, he said in accented English, 'I am afraid that we are closing for the night.'

'What? No! Issso early.'

'It's after midnight.'

Michel reached into his apron for her bill, placed it onto a round silver tray, and left it on her table. He scurried inside to retrieve the card machine.

'No unicorn stickers for you!' she called after him. Gabriel wondered why Michel would want unicorn stickers.

And then she began to cry again.

Sighing, Gabriel slammed his book closed. Michel was right to cut her off. It was dangerous to drink so much as a woman travelling alone in a foreign city. Somebody would need to protect her from herself and, annoyingly, as the only gentleman left in the bistro, it would have to be him.

He dropped the book into his satchel along with his reading glasses and left twenty euros on the table for Michel, who returned to take payment from the woman. She wiped at her face and blew her nose on one of the cloth napkins before fumbling around in her mammoth handbag for her wallet. Gabriel had always wondered how women found anything inside such big bags. He preferred an orderly bag with lots of compartments.

Gabriel stood and approached Michel, who was still waiting.

Michel flubbed his generous lips and said in French, 'What am I going to do with her? She is too drunk, and I have no idea where she's staying.'

'Well, then, today is your lucky day,' said Gabriel as he slapped him on the back, 'because I do.'

He had watched her arrive through the front window of his gallery that afternoon. His sister greeted the woman and showed her to the investment rental they ran together in the building above, a few floors below his penthouse apartment. By 'running it together', he meant that he paid the bills and his sister, Elodie, did everything else: the marketing, the cleaning, and any human interaction.

'*Dieu merci*,' Michel exclaimed. Gabriel suspected the waiter would have grabbed him by the shoulders and kissed him if Michel wasn't a full head shorter.

Finally, she found her wallet and waved the card towards the machine, missing it. Michel had to move the machine around to connect the receiver with the plastic rectangle as her hand swayed. Job done, he briskly tore off her receipt and gave it to her, saying to Gabriel, 'She's your problem now!' before practically skipping back into the restaurant.

With another deep sigh, Gabriel surveyed the scene before him.

On her table—along with her second empty bottle of red—sat two antique cookie jars. One was a pig in a chef's outfit with rosy cheeks and its tongue poking out of its mouth. The other one was uglier, a green-skinned witch with dark hair, beady obsidian eyes, a pursed mouth, and a pointed ceramic hat on her head. They were arranged on the table as though they were her dinner companions and confidantes.

Gabriel cleared his throat. 'Who are your friends?' he asked, trying to make conversation to put her at ease. He didn't want her to accuse him of being a wanker.

She turned her face up and refocused on him, eyes widening slightly as her gaze settled. Blue. Her eyes were a clear aquamarine blue, like the sky on a sunny day.

'Oh, hello again, handsome,' she said. An attractive blush pinked her cheeks as she ogled him. 'I'm Jess. This is Pierre.' She waved a manicured hand towards the pig. 'And the ugly witchy one...I call her Francesca.' She laughed at a joke that was not apparent to him, but it rapidly transformed into sobs.

'I'm Gabriel,' he said, 'let's get you back to your apartment.' He picked up her bag and slung it over his shoulder, on top of his satchel.

With sudden energy, she stood up and shouted, 'Sir! I am *not* that kind of girl!' And then she slapped his cheek hard.

Both of them blinked with shock.

'Ouch.' He rubbed at his throbbing cheek. 'What did you do that for?'

Righteously angry, she said, 'I thought you were hitting on me!' And then a little less sure: 'Weren't you?'

'I was trying to help you. My sister is your host. I was going to see you safely back to your apartment.' His skin still smarted from the impact.

Jess's hands flew to her face and tented over her nose and mouth. 'Omigod! I'm so sorry. Yes, I can see the resemblance now.'

Gabriel raised an eyebrow. He and his sister looked nothing alike, especially since his black hair had become prematurely peppered with grey.

'I'm such an idiot,' she continued. 'You see, I've never slapped anyone before, and I'm trying to be more spon...spon...spon—'

'Spontaneous?'

'Yes! That!' She tried to click her fingers and failed.

'And slapping me was spontaneous?'

She bit her lip and nodded.

Gabriel crossed his arms. 'Turning left rather than right is spontaneous. Slapping someone is assault.' He tilted his head to the side and narrowed his eyes. 'And by the way, if I was hitting on you, you'd know it.' Call him old-fashioned, but he preferred his sexual partners to be sober, willing and, most importantly, no strings attached.

Her shoulders drooped. 'I think my ex broke up with me because —because he thinks I'm too buttoned-up. You know...*boring*.' The sobs overtook her again, and she tipped towards him, leaning her forehead against his shoulder.

His nostrils filled with the scent of her shampoo. Strawberries. His favourite fruit.

'I want to go home now,' she said as her crying stopped and she pulled back, wiping under her eyes with her fingers. He glanced down at his shirt and saw two mascara marks on the linen. He was already regretting his intervention.

'Your apartment is there.' He flicked his head towards the seven-storey building next door, the uniform Juliet balconies looking south over Paris.

'I mean *home* home. Why did I come here?' Her chin sank towards her chest and something in him growled, angry to see this beautiful creature brought so low.

Against his better judgment, he reached out and lifted her chin. Her sad eyes found his, recognising a kindred spirit in pain, he supposed. 'You came because you were being spontaneous.'

Their gazes locked. He noticed a fleck of dark blue in her left eye. An island in a calm sea.

'Go on, man! Kiss her!' yelled a passing group of drunken British tourists, followed by exaggerated smoochy noises. Gabriel let go of her chin, and she swayed as though he had been holding her up. She stumbled backwards into the table.

6

Time slid into slow-motion as he watched the piggy cookie jar wobble back and forth, back and forth—before it finally tipped over the edge.

'Pierre!' she called out.

But it was too late. Pierre lay shattered on the floor.

2

J ESS LEANED AGAINST THE HALLWAY WALL WHILE THE GORGEOUS BUT
annoyingly serious stranger entered a code into a panel stuck to the
flat's door. At least the fact that he knew the code corroborated his
story about being related to her host.

She squinted at his profile. With his timeless salt-and-pepper hair
and sexy stubbled jar, she found it hard to guess his age. Somewhere
in his mid-to-late thirties? The scar across his dark eyebrow gave
him an intense, Jason Momoa look, although that's where the resemblance ended. This man had a slimmer, muscular build. Her eyes
wandered down his tall frame, past his brown loafers, and landed on
the box on the floor that contained the cookie jar formerly known as
Pierre.

Poor Pierre. She wished it had been the other one.

A whirring noise preceded his pushing the door open. He
stepped aside so that she could enter first, which made her laugh
bitterly. A gentleman like her ex, Krish.

'Thank you, er...what was your name again?'

'Gabriel.'

From the way he said it, she could tell that he'd already given her

8

this information. Embarrassed, she ducked her head as she passed him, so she wouldn't have to meet his stern brown eyes. She still couldn't believe that she'd slapped him. What must he think of her?

She thought she had sobered up considerably in the past ten minutes and now believed she could walk in a straight line without making more of a fool of herself than she already had. Even so, she kept her hand on the wall as a precautionary measure.

Her fingers glided over the light switch and she flicked it on, illuminating her quaint studio flat 'in the beating heart of Montmartre', as the write-up said. She had liked it because it was colourful, unlike many of the other options on the rental app, which were cold and crisp, decked out in sterile whites and tasteful greys. This flat felt boutique and artsy, more in line with the romantic, bohemian Paris in her head.

The man dropped her things on a square, wooden dining table and turned towards her, his expression disapproving, which made her feel chastised even though he hadn't said a word. Her brain knew she shouldn't have drunk so much while alone, but as Krish had said to her when they broke up: *'The heart wants what the heart wants.'*

And her heart had wanted two bottles of red.

Her eyes fell on a third bottle, left on the table as a welcome gift by the host.

Following her gaze, he plucked it up and plopped it in his bag. 'Not for you,' the man said.

'Hey!' she objected. 'That's stealing!'

'You'll thank me in the morning.' He went into the small kitchenette to fill a glass with water. Walking over to her spot against the wall, he thrust the drink at her. 'Here.'

He watched her guzzle it down and, with an exaggerated frown that mirrored his, she handed the empty glass back to him. He grunted with satisfaction and returned to the kitchenette to repeat the exercise.

Jess didn't like being treated like a naughty school child, espe-cially by a man with such amazing cheekbones who looked so good in linen. His physics-defying light blue shirt managed to be both loose and tight at the same time. Linen's most basic quality was that it appeared airy and breezy in all situations, and yet she clearly saw his defined pectorals. The rolled-up sleeves revealed corded fore-arms. Same with his jeans. His solid thighs were hugged by the denim. The overall effect of the whole outfit was one of sexy, easy-going comfort.

And as though that weren't enough, he had a scarf. Linen, again. Dark blue. Wrapped expertly around his neck in the way the French had mastered. A British man might have the same scarf, yet fail to achieve the same stylish look of 'Hey, I just threw this on.'

It all made her feel rather aroused.

She decided to say something intelligent. 'Did you know that I'm drinking the same water that a dinosaur peed out?' It was true. The water on earth now was exactly the same water that had been on it when the earth began. As a primary school teacher, her brain was awash with these sorts of interesting but useless facts—a quality that made her an excellent addition to any pub quiz team.

'Fascinating.' Clearly, he was unimpressed. He gave her the second full glass, and she drank it, slower this time, watching him as she swallowed. Would it kill the man to smile once in a while? She really wished he'd stop looking at her with those judgmental brown eyes. Her gaze flicked to his scarred eyebrow, which added to his generally angry countenance.

Filled with the bravery that comes from alcohol consumption, she blurted, 'How'd you get that scar?'

He reached up and touched it as though he'd forgotten it was there. 'Afghanistan,' he said, his voice devoid of emotion.

'Oh!'

Not the answer she'd expected. Had he been a soldier? Or maybe a spy? He did seem to have a talent for languages, switching between American-English and French with practised ease. Maybe those were just two of many. Maybe he was a poly-git. Poly-goblin. Poly... oh, whatever.

His scar, on top of his close affinity to linen, only added to his mystery and stoked her arousal. She had already checked his hands for a wedding ring. Nothing there. Her new motto was, *Be more spontaneous!* What could be more spontaneous than sex with a hot stranger? The double bed was only a few steps behind her under the window. That would show her ex-boyfriend. Ha!

Could she do it? She'd never had a one-night-stand before. It had always seemed too risqué for her. Plus she believed that she needed an emotional connection to take pleasure in sex. Would she enjoy making love without the love part? *If you never try, you'll never know,* she always told her class. Maybe she should follow her own advice.

But first, she had to turn that frown upside down.

'Do you ever smile?' She dropped the glass on a nearby coffee table and reached out with both pointer fingers. Time slowed as she poked them into the corners of his down-turned lips and pushed them upwards.

He regarded her with flat eyes as she manhandled his face. 'What are you doing?'

She retracted her fingers and stepped closer to him. 'Just checking the muscles worked.' She smelled the subtle scent of his cologne: woodsy and spicy. Masculine. Completely the opposite of Krish, who always smelled a bit too lemony for her liking.

'Why?'

'So I can do this.' Jess launched herself at the man, taking his head between her hands, and plonking her lips onto his. She expected him to pull her towards him passionately—French men were always up for it, right?—but instead, he placed his hands on her hips and pushed away.

'I don't think so.'

Embarrassment rushed through her. What seemed like a great plan only a second ago, now revealed itself to be the worst idea ever. What had she just done—accosting this poor stranger like a pigeon in heat? She didn't even know his name. Or did she?

'I'm-I'm sorry.' She covered her eyes with her hands. Maybe if she didn't look, then it didn't happen.

He had already started backing towards the door. 'Much as I applaud your spontaneity science fair project, I'm not sure I want to be Exhibit A. So I'm going to say *bonne nuit* and...I suggest you take some painkillers before you hit the sack. Have a wonderful time in Paris.'

With that, he departed, and the lock clicked closed. Jess had never seen a man run away from her so fast.

Blood rushed to her face and she bonked her fist against her forehead. 'Jess, you idiot!' This was why she didn't like getting drunk. It made her act out of character and do stupid things. She'd definitely remember that for next time.

She blamed Krish. Her heart clenched at the thought of him, still acclimating to the fact that he would no longer be in her life. She missed him. And she hated him. And she loved him. Tonight, they were supposed to be having dinner at some over-priced French restaurant on the Seine. Instead, she'd gone to a flea market, ate *Steak Frites* to line her stomach, and then drowned her sorrows in cheap wine.

Speaking of her stomach, it decided to add to her problems, as nausea climbed through her torso up towards her mouth. Her heart may have wanted two bottles of wine, but her stomach had not been consulted.

Almost as fast as Gabriel had backed out of the flat, Jess bolted for the toilet.

A HOT BEAM of morning sunlight tickled Jess's nose.

She groaned and peeked at her watch.

Scratch that. A hot beam of *afternoon* sunlight tickled Jess's nose. It was already 1PM.

Jess swore and threw off her covers. No way she would waste another minute in Paris. She leapt out of bed and immediately regretted it. The dizziness hit her fast, and she had to grab a chair to remain standing. She froze for a minute, waiting for her swirling head to settle. She noticed the box containing Pierre's remnants and had a vague memory of knocking him off a table. Poor Pierre. She narrowed her eyes at Francesca the Witch, sitting whole and undamaged next to the box. The desire to tip the witch onto the floor momentarily occupied her, but she pushed it aside. The ceramic was innocent. Jess wasn't sure why she'd even bought it—probably the same human instinct for self-torture that motivated people to listen to sad songs after a break-up.

Her dizziness abated, and Jess was amazed to realise that she didn't have a throbbing headache, a small miracle because she never usually drank that much alcohol. Twelve hours of sleep, gallons of water, and the painkillers she'd taken before bed seemed to have helped her dodge the hangover bullet. Her stomach growled, reminding her that it had been empty for some time.

She'd come off lightly from her heartbreak-induced bender, with a broken pig as the only collateral damage. Well, she could check getting drunk in Paris off of her bucket list and move on to actual tourist activities. She was determined to have some new experiences on this trip. Keeping busy was the order of the day, so she didn't have time to think about what she'd be doing if Krish were here, or whether she'd always been second best in his heart. She shook her head to dislodge the negative thoughts.

Desperate for hydration, she stepped towards the kitchenette, and a memory shoved into her mind. A man. Salt and pepper hair. Glasses of water. Cheekbones to die for and a sensual mouth. Kissing his soft, but unyielding lips and the faint taste of cognac.

Her stomach dropped and she squeezed her eyes tightly shut. 'Oh my god, Jess. You idiot.'

Who was that man? In her head, flashes of her interactions with him assailed her, ending with the poor man backing away from her, eyes averted, like her hair had turned to snakes. How utterly horrifying.

Whomever he was, she appreciated his help. She had been stupid to drink so much in a strange city, and she was well aware that it had been a bad idea.

If she ever saw him again, she'd thank him.

But she hoped she'd never see him again.

In the kitchenette, she poured herself a glass of water and glugged it down. With her bottom leaning against the counter, she surveyed the bijou flat that she had rented for six nights after extending her return date from Sunday to Thursday. She didn't have to be at school to set up her classroom until next week, so why rush back? There was nobody waiting for her there.

Her heart pinched with sadness. She wondered for the millionth time what she had done wrong and why Krish had dumped her for another woman. And for the millionth time, no answers came to her. Even though he was apologetic and explained that his feelings for Francesca were irrepressible, she still wondered if she could have done something to keep him with her. Maybe that time he asked if he could tie her to the bed during sex, she should have said yes. Given it a go.

Making it even worse, she had a history of being dumped. The few boyfriends she'd had before Krish had also ended things first. She'd never been the one to walk away.

What was wrong with her?

Then again, maybe there had always been a disconnect between Krish and her, and she'd just never noticed it because everything on the surface worked well. For example, their taste in hotels. Krish had booked them a room at the infamous George V, notably the finest hotel in Paris.

Jess never would have chosen that place. Yesterday, pulling her shabby TK Maxx suitcase across the shiny marble floor, she'd walked alone into the opulent lobby, which was decked out in fresh flowers and smelled of expensive perfume. To her right, a Middle Eastern family of four dressed in matching white Gucci track suits were sitting on chairs as though awaiting their turn to compete in the wealth olympics. While the mother and kids concentrated on their top-of-the-range iPhones, the father was forcefully explaining to one of the hotel employees exactly how and in which spot he would like his Lamborghini parked. His patronising tone rubbed Jess up the wrong way, having been on the receiving end of it from some parents at the private school where she worked.

If coming to Paris alone was her first spontaneous act, then turning around and leaving the Hotel George V had been her second. That place and its people were not her vibe. Krish was the one who liked expensive hotels and fancy restaurants; she had simpler tastes. Jess pulled out her phone, downloaded a flat rental app, and found a place that was more her style.

And this place definitely was her style. It was small, one room that contained the kitchen, dining area, and bedroom. She liked that. To her, it felt like a warm hug. The walls were painted a deep red, and none of the furniture matched. Not a stick of Ikea in sight. Across from her bed, two tall wooden bookshelves were crammed with books whose spines were losing colour from baking in the sun.

A mix of French and English authors existed side by side in no apparent order. A librarian's worst nightmare. Shakespeare lived next to Colette. Isaac Asimov beside Jules Verne. She was surprised to see a well-thumbed Jilly Cooper novel on there. Jess loved a bit of Jilly.

Next to the bookcases, a collection of random ceramic dishware lined shelves above the dining table built for two. Thin gold lines crisscrossed the cups and bowls as though somebody had painstakingly reassembled them using metallic glue. The effect was delicately beautiful. Jess bit her lip, feeling a strange kinship with those broken dishes. She hoped to find some golden glue on this trip to put herself back together again.

Stop being melodramatic, she thought and stood straighter. She was in Paris.

And she was going to have a good time.

3

STEPPING OUT OF THE BUILDING'S FRONT DOOR, JESS KNEW THAT SHE looked like a Hollywood starlet.

She had packed for a proposal weekend, so she didn't have a lot of casual clothes, although she had thought to bring jeans and trainers, just in case.

However, that wasn't what she chose to wear today. Today she wore the outfit that she was supposed to get engaged in: a 1950's style white dress patterned with big red flowers. The upper half hugged her torso and made her boobs look fabulous, and the bottom half flared out in an A-line, like something out of *Mad Men*. She paired them with flat red sandals. She was already tall enough and didn't find high heels comfortable at all.

The August heat simmered in the air. Only a few fluffy clouds meandered through the sky. Her street wasn't in the main tourist throng of Montmartre, nor was it a quiet backstreet. Couples wandered past, tour books in hand, searching for the Sacre Coeur or the Wall of Love—both places she had wanted to visit with Krish. A familiar hollowness expanded in her chest.

No! She slammed her mental guard down against thinking about

17

Krish and the trip she should be having. She'd bottle up her sadness for London. She hadn't even told her friends about the break-up, so she wouldn't receive pity texts throughout this trip. There would be time for being Poor Jess when she got home. Now was the time for exploration and new experiences.

Besides, a small part of her hoped that Krish would text to say it had all been a big mistake. Her logical brain knew he wouldn't; he'd made it pretty clear that, even though he loved Jess, he loved somebody else more. But hope is a stupid thing. It doesn't listen to logic.

Jess headed up the hill towards the Place du Tertre, the square where the artists hung out. Her stomach grumbled, reminding her that she'd treated it badly last night. On the way, she marvelled at the intentional beauty of everything around her: the quirky, colourful houses with lush greenery out front; the cobblestones laid in perfect fan shapes; the distinctive Parisian font on the blue street signs; and the stylish, art deco lampposts. From below her feet to the tippy top of the buildings she passed, the details had been carefully crafted. It had been somebody's job to devise a remarkable lamppost. The French understood beauty at a microscopic level.

She smiled as the huff and puff of a distant accordion reached her ears. Even the air sounded French.

Entering the square, she ambled to the red awning of La Mère Catherine, the oldest restaurant in the vicinity according to her guidebook, and nabbed an outside table. She loved people watching. And there were plenty of them here; she estimated a three-to-one ratio of tourists versus locals trying to sell crap to tourists. She observed the artists beseeching passers-by to sit for a portrait. Most said no. The ones who said yes were perched on wonky stools, attempting to hold still while pencil lines appeared on the artist's paper. Jess had no desire to have her portrait drawn. She'd spent enough time as Krish's personal photography model over the past two years, and she was done with it.

A waiter interrupted her reverie, and Jess ordered a healthy salad with an unhealthy Coca-Cola to give her a sugar boost. She didn't usually drink fizzy drinks, but Coke was a necessity after a binge like the one she'd had last night.

Her *salade niçoise* was exactly what she needed. She practically felt the vitamins rushing through her body to replenish what she'd lost.

As she paid for her lunch, a short, balding artist with thick black glasses caught her eye from his stand on the outer edge of the square and rushed over. '*Mademoiselle*, I make a picture for you now, *oui?*'

'No,' she said with a kind tilt of her head. 'Not today, *merci*.' She wanted to explore, not sit in a chair for an hour. She stood up and stepped around him.

Another artist wearing an actual beret came over. 'Forget him, *mademoiselle*. He is—how you say?—a hack. Please, I create silhouette of you.' As his scissors started working at the black paper in his hands, she noticed that his eyes were trained on her breasts.

The first artist said something sharp to the second one, and they began to argue.

Two artists fighting over a model...this also seemed very French —although it made her feel distinctly uncomfortable. She slipped away before things escalated, wondering if they would have been so bold if Krish were at her side. She dismissed the thought of him again.

Heading towards the Sacre Coeur, the famous white basilica that towered over Paris, she reached into her bag to find her sunglasses. Now that she was leaving the relative shade of the square and side streets, the mid-afternoon sun blazed in the sky, forcing her to squint. Jess patted around inside her bag, but couldn't locate the hard case.

She slapped her forehead as a picture of her sunglasses sitting on the table in her flat formed in her mind. She could just go on without them...but then she thought of her parents, who both had cataracts and had warned her repeatedly against the dangers of ocular sun exposure.

Jess sighed. Some risks were just too big to take. Like the good daughter she was, she spun around and walked back through the square and down the hill. As she approached her building, she noticed the gallery that formed the ground floor for the first time. A large framed photograph of the Eiffel Tower taken from the sky dominated the display window. Jess stopped to admire the image's beauty, the way the yellow paths in the park surrounding the tower looped like ticker tapes, permanently frozen in celebration. On a whim, she decided to go in and look around.

A bell tinkled as she pushed the door open. No shop assistant greeted her, but a gruff male voice called out something in French. The same voice repeated in English: 'We're closing soon.' She assumed said voice was coming from the storage room behind the empty back desk. Through the door, she saw shelves stacked with boxes of varying sizes, but no person.

The space had a gallery feel to it: clean white walls and directional lighting to emphasise the artwork. The pictures took her breath away—all shot from the air. Some were discernible Parisian landmarks: the Arc de Triomphe, Notre Dame, and the Louvre. But others were more abstract, from other parts of France. A river snaking through a forest. A close-up of a disintegrating coastline. Waves breaking off the coast of Normandy. Jess thought of her great-grandfather, who had fought in World War II and survived the invasion at Normandy Beach. He had died a long time ago; she only had vague memories of an old man with paper skin and liver spots who smelled of menthol and coughed a lot. She wished she'd been old enough to talk to him about his experiences. Nobody in her family had written down his story. All that history, lost.

'Well, if it isn't Sleeping Beauty,' said a deep, smug voice.

Jess jumped, torn out of her thoughts. She turned her head and found herself looking at a familiar face. For a moment, she felt like she'd been there before, in this gallery, wearing this dress, meeting this person with his distinguished salt and pepper hair, judgemental frown, and scar. The sensation passed, and she snapped back into her present timeline, a dizzy feeling of unreality lingering and then slowly fading away.

'It's you! Er...' Did she know his name? Blood rushed to her cheeks as the few memories she did have from the previous night needled her again. Her toes curled with awkward self-conscious-ness, especially as she realised that her brain hadn't accurately recalled just how gorgeous he really was. It was a small comfort that his eyes also swept up and down her body with reciprocal appre-ciation.

'Gabriel.' He lifted his eyebrows as though thinking she should know his name and shook his head in a patronising manner. *This woman is a lush and a danger to humanity*, it said to her. He hoisted a camera bag onto the desk and unzipped the main compartment. He inspected the lenses one by one, in a way that she had seen Krish do many times before.

'So you're a photographer.' She couldn't help how her voice dipped down as though accusing him of something nefarious. *So you're Jack the Ripper.* She'd already had her fill of photographers. Her break-up with Krish had left her somewhat camera shy. Unconsciously, she stepped back towards the door.

'Guilty as charged,' he mumbled, absorbed in his task.

Her head told her to go and she took another step towards the exit, but stopped herself. Despite his career choice, she didn't want him to think badly of her for last night, even if he was a sullen grouch. But how did one apologise to a stranger for making an unwanted, drunken advance? The room went quiet for a moment. She grappled for the right thing to say while studying a picture of Les Invalides, where Napoleon's Tomb rested. He, on the other hand, seemed in no hurry to talk to her, involved as he was in prepping his kit.

Here goes nothing. Clearing her throat, she smiled her sweetest smile and said, 'Thank you for your help, by the way. Last night, I mean. I don't usually get drunk like that. It was just—'

'The break-up. I know,' he said without looking up, his voice implying that she had told him quite enough. He loaded a memory card into the back of his camera.

How much did he know? Her old friend embarrassment turned up again, and she scuffed at a non-existent mark on the floor with her foot.

'Still,' he began as he replaced his camera in the bag. 'It's irresponsible to get so drunk when you're travelling alone.'

Her mouth fell open. Jess resented his admonishing tone, which for some reason was even more galling in an American accent. Who did he think he was? Her dad? She already knew it was a bad idea, but hated hearing him say it. Twinned feelings of shame and annoyance danced through her. She was a grown woman and could make her own choices, even the bad ones.

With an uncharacteristic trace of sarcasm, she said, 'Well, I guess I'll just be grateful that you were around to save me.'

For some reason, his arrogant features froze, and a stricken look crossed his face. His forehead crumpled, his gaze turning inward. A few long seconds passed before he visibly shook himself and resumed zipping up the bag with unnecessary vigour, his lips pressed into a thin line.

What was *that* about?

She cast around for something else to say, feeling awkward. 'Your work is beautiful.'

'Thanks,' he practically grunted.

The man was obviously busy. She was about to say her farewells and leave when her phone beeped to alert her to a new text. She fished it out of her bag. It was a message from Krish! Perhaps he'd had a chance to think about it some more and realised that he'd made an awful mistake.

With a hopeful smile, she opened it and read:

> Hey Jess, All okay? I'm worried about you being all alone in Paris. I can't begin to tell you how sorry I am that I hurt you. Krish x

Her illogical hope finally died. Her chest filled with a cottony feeling, and a sob escaped her mouth. Hot tears formed in her eyes. Checking up on her was a very Krish thing to do, but it just opened wounds that she had sewn closed using weak thread. She wished he'd just leave her be. With a trembling finger, she blocked his number.

A tissue appeared in front of her, held out by Gabriel, who had an even angrier scowl than usual on his face. 'Was that Chris?' he asked.

'Krish, yes,' she corrected him.

'What a dick move. He should leave you alone.'

For some reason she felt the urge to stick up for her ex, even though Gabriel's sentiments echoed hers. Despite the fact that things had ended unexpectedly, Krish had been the perfect boyfriend up until that point. She'd struggle to find anybody with the same myth-ical combination of kindness, sexiness, and ambition. The thought made her well up again. 'Actually, he was one of the good ones. That's why I'm so upset.'

Gabriel snorted. 'Obviously not, if he was stupid enough to walk away from you.'

In light of their conversation so far, his words surprised her, shocking her tears into drying up. Their eyes met for a moment: blue on brown. The scar across his right eyebrow gave his gaze a degree of extra intensity. She looked away first.

She used the tissue he'd given her to clean up the last wet marks from her face. With Gabriel standing so close, she caught his scent, which she surprisingly remembered from last night. It made her think of snuggling by a roaring fire on a cold winter's day.

'Sorry,' she said, 'it's still a bit raw.' She tried not to picture what she and Krish would be doing right now in the alternate reality where he hadn't broken her heart. Walking along the Seine, gazing into each other's eyes…

Cutting into her thoughts, Gabriel said, 'Are you still doing the spontaneous thing?' He crossed his arms.

Jess blew her nose into the tissue and tucked it into her pocket. She loved a dress with pockets for just this very reason. 'Yes?'

He cocked his head to the side, and she was struck again by how good-looking he was. Gabriel asked, 'Have you ever been in a helicopter?'

'No…why?' She could just about handle going on an airplane. She also hated rollercoasters and hot air balloons. Basically anything where the distance between her and the earth was unnaturally exaggerated.

He narrowed his eyes and then shook his head. 'Nah, never mind. It was a stupid idea.'

Now she wanted to know. 'No! Tell me…please.' She touched him, laying her palm over his forearm. She didn't expect how her hand tingled in reaction, so she jerked it away. She hoped he didn't notice her blush.

Hesitating, he pursed his lips. She tilted her head and blinked with beggar's eyes to encourage him. Finally, he sighed and said, 'Well, I'm going up in a helicopter this afternoon. Shooting from the air.' He turned and crossed back towards the desk; she noticed he had a very confident, assured stride. Over his shoulder, he said, 'There's room for one more…but you probably don't want to do it.'

'Yes, I do!' *No, you don't.* She could already feel a fine bead of sweat gathering at the back of her neck. Why was she pursuing this?

It reminded her of young Jess, and the time she was dying to eat dinner at her friend's house. The friend asked her mum if Jess could stay, and the mother said, 'You can, but we're having liver. Do you like liver?' Knowing full well that she absolutely detested liver, Jess waxed poetic about her love of the stuff. She stayed for dinner and wanted to gag the whole time.

But this had higher stakes than a dinner; this was trusting somebody she didn't know with her life. On the other hand, he was offering her a new experience. In school, they taught the kids to have a growth mindset, which involved putting *Yet* on the end of phrases. *I can't spell..yet! I can't read...yet!* It helped the children understand that life was a journey and things they couldn't do today were possible tomorrow.

She thought, *I haven't died in a helicopter...yet!*

For some reason, that failed to convince her.

Another question surfaced: 'Why would you do this for me?' she asked. He was a total stranger. Did he have ulterior motives? If that were the case, surely he would have taken advantage of her last night. Besides, she didn't get a creepy vibe off him, like she did with the artists. But still...

He quickly glanced to the side as though he wasn't sure himself. 'Let's just say I'm paying it forward.'

Their eyes held for a moment, but this time, he looked away first. *There's a story there*, she thought. *I wonder what he's paying forward.* Of course, she wouldn't ask. It was none of her business.

That only left one question: should she go?

Jess bit her lip. She didn't want to spend her whole life playing it safe. And this was her chance to do something that would push her out of her comfort zone—like, *so far out* of her comfort zone that she'd need the aid of a satellite to communicate with it. She imagined Krish's reaction if she told him she'd done this. He'd be shocked.

Well, she'd show him. She could be adventurous.

Puffing out her chest, she said with more confidence than she felt, 'Let's do it. Will we get nicknames? Like in *Top Gun*?' If yes, she wanted to be Boudicca.

Gabriel shook his head as though they'd just agreed to the terms of a hostile corporate takeover and he was the losing party. 'Why do I already feel like I'm going to regret this?'

4

As the taxi sped towards the heliport, Gabriel questioned his common sense for the hundredth time since inviting Jess on this excursion. Selfless acts of this sort weren't usually his thing. In fact, he tried to avoid unnecessary interactions with other humans as much as possible. It was easier for him that way. Today just had to be the day that his gallery manager called in sick.

But then Jess had walked in looking like a couture Venus and broken down in tears when her shit ex-boyfriend texted her. Something inside of Gabriel twisted, and that voice inside his head that sounded like Fatima said: *don't be a douche. You have the power to do something special for her*—and then the invitation came out of his mouth. If there was one voice he couldn't disobey, it was Fatima's.

What was the worst that could happen? He'd brought along his sister, Elodie, on the last one, and she'd loved it. Jess's rental booking was only for six days and, if he could help take her mind off the asshole who'd dumped her, then why not? To be completely honest with himself—and after years of therapy he always tried to be—he could use some distraction at the moment, too.

Guess I'll be part of her Spontaneity Science Fair Project after all, he thought.

The ride would be chilly, so he gave her instructions on how to dress, which unfortunately didn't involve the incredible outfit she had on. Her legs seemed to go on forever and the uninvited image of them wrapped around his waist flashed across his imagination. He boxed the image up and dropped it into his internal delete bin.

They parted ways for half an hour and, when they reconvened, she was wearing figure-hugging blue jeans, a newly-bought pink sweatshirt that said *'Paris je t'aime'*, and a pair of white sneakers. He advised her to braid her long blonde hair to keep it from flying around in the wind.

To be fair, Gabriel was surprised she'd turned up at all. He recognised the idea of flying in a helicopter scared the living crap out of her, even though she had that big scintillating smile pasted across her face. She kept wringing her hands and tugging on her braid like it was a lifeline. He also heard her muttering, 'You can do this, Jess. You can do this.' Secretly, he thought it was kind of adorable. And he admired that she was willing to try. He knew from experience that bravery could be a quiet series of gutsy small decisions. It didn't have to be a big heroic act.

He also knew that this would be a once-in-a-lifetime experience for her. It gave him a surprising warm glow that he could give her this. That same unwelcome voice in his head said: *see? I knew you hadn't turned into a complete asshole.* Shifting in his seat, he immediately tamped down the glow. Gabriel wasn't doing this for gratitude or accolades. He was doing it because…because she seemed a little lost and he understood that. It was a one-off thing and she'd be gone in a few days. It wasn't like she'd grow attached to him or anything.

The shoot had been planned for months. Getting permits to fly above Paris required a masters degree in bureaucracy, which he completely lacked. Thankfully, he had an old colleague in the prefecture of police who let him complete two flights of 45 minutes each per year in exchange for using the images on social media and exhibitions in a few public buildings (plus a modest kickback from sales). Other cities around the world were much less restrictive about air space, but the French...if they could make something difficult, then they would. Stubborn to the core. And he said that as a stubborn Frenchman himself. He always thought the famous motto should be amended to: Liberté, égalité, fraternité, *obstiné*.

But today's shoot was even more unique because they were heading out to Versailles, which had required another round of special permissions. His agent had done the negotiating. The authorities stressed that they hadn't given a photographer consent to do aerial shots of Versailles since Yann Arthus-Bertrand.

The pilot, Jacques, was one he had worked with several times. They had established a shorthand between them long ago: Gabriel would ask for what he wanted—a steep bank, tight orbits over a particular landmark—and Jacques would manoeuvre the helicopter in the safest way possible to deliver it. Gabriel would never question Jacques' choices. Safety was paramount. No risks.

They'd gone over the map and discussed what Gabriel wanted to achieve on this expedition. All he needed to do now was get the shots.

JESS WATCHED Paris whoosh by through the taxi window, her foot tapping on the floor. All she could think about were stories she had heard in the news of helicopters crashing, and it didn't help when Gabriel asked her: 'Do you have any experience with increased G-force?'

'No,' she said with saucer eyes.

He made a dismissive motion with his hand. 'Don't worry. It'll only be three to four Gs, max. You'll be fine.'

But she did worry. She worried about a lot of things, including not seeming grateful despite the fact she was doubting her own sanity right now. 'I just wanted to say thank you, by the way. It was really kind of you to invite me along.' *Even if I might be driving towards my death,* she added.

Gabriel shrugged and grumbled, 'I didn't do it to be kind. I did it…because you seemed like you needed help. And I was in a position to help you. That's all.'

Well, in her book, that was being kind, even if he didn't want to call it that for some reason. 'Thank you anyway.' She needed to keep talking, to take her mind off the fact that she was about to get in a helicopter and experience Gs with a strange man. 'So, Gabriel, tell me: are you French or American? Or both?'

'I'm French, but I spent my teen years in New Jersey. My father worked for a pharmaceutical company, and he was transferred to their US HQ when I was twelve.'

Jess had spent her whole life in the countryside around Bristol in the same house since birth, even studying at the university there. Moving to London after graduating had been a huge leap for her. 'Wow, that must have been an experience.'

'It was. Although I had to survive almost ten years of being called Gabe.' He made a sour face, and she laughed, partly out of surprise that he could be funny. The corners of his mouth flickered upwards —so quick, she almost missed it.

Jess decided it would be her goal to make him laugh before the day was out. 'Was it strange when you returned to France?'

'A bit. I came back after studying photojournalism in DC. But then I started working almost straight away, so I was on the move a lot.'

'Working as…?'

He was quiet for a beat. 'A war photographer.'

'Oh.' Her eyes shot to his scar.

He turned towards the window. 'We're here.'

Her head whipped forward, and she saw they were pulling into the heliport. The taxi stopped outside a hangar with corrugated metal walls and a white cathedral roof. In front of it sat a gleaming blue helicopter sparkling in the sun. She gulped hard.

Gabriel retrieved his camera bag from the boot and helped her out of the car. She couldn't take her eyes off the helicopter. Something about it wasn't quite right…

'Why aren't there any doors? GABRIEL?' She grabbed his arm. 'Where are the doors?!'

'How would I take pictures if there were doors?' he said as though she were being unreasonable. She couldn't see his eyes behind his mirrored aviator sunglasses, but from the tone in his voice, she imagined they were shining with quiet amusement.

Her heart knocked in her chest.

Noting her distress, he said, 'Don't worry. It really is safe. I've done at least fifty of these trips all over the world.'

She distrusted when people used the fact that they'd done a dangerous act loads of times to infer that it was perfectly safe. Had he never heard of *accidents*?

'You can still pull out,' he said gently. He slipped his sunglasses down his nose and dipped down a little so that he caught her eye.

The idea tempted her. It didn't matter if she chose not to go up. Nobody would lose any money. The trip would still go ahead. But she would know that she'd had a choice between adventure and cowardice, and she'd chosen the wrong one.

'No, I want to come with you.'

'Great. Good.' A moment passed. 'Um, do you mind releasing my arm?' he said.

Jess looked down and realised she still had his forearm in a vise.

She unclasped and watched as he jiggled it to encourage blood flow. 'Sorry.'

He shook his head and led the way towards the hulking blue machine. The pilot was examining the helicopter, marking off items on a laminated pre-flight checklist. That assuaged Jess's fears a little; at least the pilot seemed responsible. His appearance further heartened her: reassuringly middle-aged with the beer belly to prove it. The calm, systematic way he inspected his helicopter reminded her of how her dad checked her bike every time before she was allowed to ride it. Tires—pumped. Chain—greased. Bolts—tightened.

Gabriel waited until the pilot had finished before approaching him to say hello. They did one of those man handshakes where, instead of clasping them together like normal people, they looked like they were about to arm wrestle, followed by a double slap on the shoulder.

Afterwards, Gabriel introduced Jess. She held her hand out and Jacques pulled her in for a French *bise*—the traditional kiss on the cheek. He laughed at her surprise and said something foreign. When Jess looked at Gabriel for a translation, he just said: '*Anglaise.*'

'Ahhh,' said Jacques, and he regarded her with the same look one might give to someone who announced she had a terminal disease.

Recovering from his disappointment, Jacques handed her a form to sign, where she had to write down her next of kin details. As she filled in her dad's mobile number, she thought how upset her parents would be if they knew what she was doing. The riskiest thing they did was eating vegetables past their use-by date. If they could see her now, they would wonder if she'd suffered a head injury.

Next, the pilot took them through a health and safety briefing with Gabriel translating. He reminded her not to bring any loose items, to stay in her seat, to avoid the rotors if walking around the aircraft—as if she needed to be told—and described how to exit safely in the event of a crash.

'Crash?' she repeated, her voice rising an octave in one word.

'It's okay,' said Gabriel. 'They have to tell us that. Jacques has racked up over one thousand flights. He used to fly for the French Air Force. You'll be fine.' He nudged her with his shoulder and she huffed a humourless laugh. 'Jess. Look at me.' He took off his sunglasses with one hand and lifted her chin with the other in a way she vaguely remembered from the night before. Her gaze dropped briefly to his lips, and she recalled the feeling of them on hers, however quick it had been. Her breath caught. 'You'll. Be. Fine.'

She couldn't tear her eyes away from his—dependable, solid, sober brown eyes. He had a maturity and gravitas that made her trust him. *Krish is just a boy compared with him.* The thought came out of nowhere.

Jess exhaled shakily. 'Okay.'

Dropping his hand, he glanced left and right. 'Can I tell you a secret?' She nodded and he leaned towards her: 'I'm actually afraid of heights.'

Pulling back, she smiled. 'No way.'

'Absolutely terrified. Ever since I was a kid.' He pointed towards the sky. 'But I don't feel it when I'm up there. There's so much beauty...well, you'll see.'

Her dad had a book about confronting fear on his shelf. Curious, she'd read through it, but disagreed with the basic idea of making people do things that scared them. It seemed simplistic and irre-sponsible. They were scared for a reason, right? But in this moment, the title phrase came back to her. She recalled one part that said if she took more risks, then it would exercise her resilience to baseless fear, making her open to new experiences.

Well, this was a new experience. An opportunity that would never come up again. And she didn't want to let her fear stop her.

'I can *do* this.' She curled her hands into determined fists.

Once, a student asked her if a person or animal could die from fear. '*Nothing can actually die from being scared,*' she had told him with conviction.

But then she'd looked it up, and there was something called Takotsubo Cardiomyopathy, when emotional or physical distress could trigger a heart incident. And it affected more women than men.

The knowledge made her shiver. Jess swallowed and concentrated on her shoes.

I'll be fine.

I'll be fine.

I'll be fine.

Gabriel touched her arm. She jumped. From how he looked at her, she wondered if he had been calling her name for a while. He asked if she needed anything before they got in. She wanted to say yes, a Valium, but she just shook her head. He took her bag and his camera backpack and disappeared into the hangar while Jacques invited her to climb into the cabin. Still wary, she kept her feet on the ground and peered inside like a forensic engineer sniffing out weaknesses. Two straight-backed leather seats took up half the cabin while the other half was a jigsaw of locked compartments, like in the galley on commercial flights where they stored the food. On this aircraft, she hoped those compartments hid lots and lots of parachutes.

Jacques cleared his throat and said, '*Mademoiselle?*', which she translated to, 'Get in the bloody helicopter, lady.'

Sucking in a deep breath, she counted to three and launched herself inside, startling Jacques, who had to take a step back. She threw herself onto the chair furthest from the door—or lack of door —and Jacques fixed a harness around her that secured her to the seat in multiple places. She tugged on it roughly after he fastened it, just to make sure it wouldn't come off. Jacques watched her with amusement.

'*C'est bon?*' he asked with a thumbs up. She gulped and nodded yes.

Gabriel returned, carrying only his camera. He handed it up to her, and she took it in her gently trembling hands, placing the heavy weight on her lap. The sight of another helicopter landing a few hangars over distracted her. She stared at the way it hovered and then touched down once, twice, three times before settling safely on the ground. Helicopters seemed like such flimsy things upon further inspection.

When she turned back, Gabriel was already in his seat, with Jacques securing the harness. Gabriel was asking questions, and the pilot, replying *oui* a lot. Hearing Gabriel speak French did unexpected, funny things to her nether regions. Focusing on his mouth, she noted that it moved differently when he spoke French. His cheekbones somehow became more pronounced and his lips pushed forward and appeared more rounded.

For a second, she wondered what it would be like to kiss his French mouth properly. With tongues and everything.

Whoa. She drew back and averted her wide eyes. Where had that come from? Her body was obviously mistaking fear for sexual arousal. Besides, the man seemed to barely tolerate her, and she had just been dumped. Shouldn't her sex drive be wearing black and avoiding public engagements?

Jacques finished clipping Gabriel in and climbed into the cockpit. As an added safety measure, she tugged on her harness again. It seemed secure. She reached over and yanked on Gabriel's harness, too. She didn't want him to fall out, either.

'Feel better now?' he asked, his frown back in place. 'Don't worry, I'm a qualified skydiver.'

'You're kidding, right?'

'Let's hope we don't need to find out.'

'That's not funny.'

He took the camera off her lap, looping the strap around his neck and depositing the lens cap and his sunglasses in a zipped pocket inside his leather coat. As he pulled his hand out again, he had two wrapped candies in his palm.

'Do you want one? It's ginger. To help with the nausea.'

'Nausea?' she repeated like she had never heard the word before.

'Just in case,' he winked at her.

She wished he had given her all the information before tempting her on this magical mystery tour. G-force, nausea...? Next thing, he'd tell her they were going to fly upside-down. She shuddered and took the candy, popping it in her mouth while giving him the side eye.

Jacques handed them each a headset, and she clamped it on. Jess bobbled her head around in all directions to ensure the headset stayed in place, moving her chin in a figure-8, left and right, up and down.

Gabriel contemplated her with an amused glint in his eyes. 'You remind me of a cat that's just had a cone fitted around its neck.' His voice sounded tinny through the headphones.

'Ha ha ha.' Feeling cheeky, she stuck her tongue out at him.

And he laughed!

Jess gaped at him with shock and surprise, like he'd just turned into a unicorn. His eyes crinkled, and his cheeks creased. His smile banished serious Gabriel to an alternate dimension.

'What?' he said, the corners of his mouth still lifted.

She shook her head. 'Frankly, I didn't know you had it in you.'

He rolled his eyes. 'I know how to smile. I just don't feel like it most of the time.'

Before she could answer, the helicopter bubbled to life. The blades rotated above them: whoosh, whoosh, whoosh. Something beeped and Jess jolted, grabbing onto Gabriel's arm.

'What was that?'

'Nothing. It's normal,' said Gabriel with a grin. His excitement animated him. 'There are going to be beeps and noises. If there's a problem—which there won't be—Jacques will tell us.'

Jess nodded and sucked on the sweet extra hard.

Moments later, the helicopter lifted off the ground, and she gasped. Squeezing her eyes shut, Jess threaded her arm through Gabriel's like he had transformed into a buoyancy device.

He covered her hand with his and she absorbed his calming warmth. 'You'll be fine. I've got you,' he said, and he sounded so sure. A very, very, very, very small part of her relaxed.

And then the helicopter zoomed into the sky.

5

THE GROUND SANK AWAY AND THE WIND SLAPPED ACROSS HER FACE
through the open doors. The hangar that had seemed so huge a
moment ago dwindled until it was the size of a garden shed. Gabriel
tapped her arm and pointed. In the distance, she saw the Eiffel
Tower, soaring up from the skyline. It glinted in the late afternoon
light and she held her breath. It was beautiful.

Jess smiled.

The helicopter veered away and she lost sight of the iron tower.

All of Paris spread out before her, a well-ordered crisscross of
buildings and roads broken up by the occasional green space. The
geometric patterns of circles, squares and rectangles revealed themselves to her, and Jess marvelled at how neat and organised it looked
from above.

'Almost like it was planned,' she said, comparing it with the disor-
derly mess of London, viewed many times in the opening title of
Eastenders.

'It *was* planned,' said Gabriel, his voice coming through the headphones, making the tiny hairs in her inner ear stand to attention. She
realised that she was leaning her arms on his left leg so she could

look down, and she quickly righted herself, throwing him an apologetic smile. He continued, 'By a man named Georges-Eugène Haussmann.' She enjoyed how he flipped from American to French pronunciation so fluidly. 'He redesigned the city in the mid-nineteenth century. Tore down all the old medieval buildings and rebuilt Paris with long avenues that connected park to park. He used cream stone for consistency. The city itself is a work of art.'

She had to agree. Paris seemed like a massive child's logic puzzle, like the ones she used to do with pre-schoolers before her current job—where they had to take all the different-shaped pieces and fit them together to create a giant square. Each shape in its place.

Raising her eyes to the sky, her gaze fixed on one of the few clouds floating in the blue expanse. It reminded her of a child's drawing: with a flat bottom and fluffy rounded top, similar to the clouds on Andy's wallpaper in *Toy Story*.

'They look like cartoons!' She hooted with delight. She noticed Gabriel studying her with a lift at the corner of his mouth. 'What?'

'Nothing,' he replied. 'I'm just glad you're enjoying it.'

It took her a second to realise that he was right. She *was* enjoying it. She hadn't thought about her fear since she laid eyes on the Eiffel Tower.

Gabriel tapped her on the leg to get her attention. 'Do you want to touch a cloud?' he asked.

'Really?' She sounded like her class when they found out Santa was coming to visit. Her kids would be so amazed when she told them this story.

He said something in French to Jacques.

Next thing she knew, they were heading towards a small wispy cloud nearby, the only one for miles. Jacques approached with the fluffy white mass on the right of the helicopter, where she and Gabriel sat.

'Ready?' Gabriel asked. He took her hand and held it outside of the aircraft, her fingers nestled in his. Her skin blazed where they touched, in contrast to the cold, wet air as they plunged into the cloud.

For a moment, moist greyness surrounded them on one side, but when she looked out the other door, she still saw blue skies. They were skimming the edge of the cloud. She laughed and turned her palm vertical, wanting to feel more; his hand moved with hers. Sailing the air in sync.

Just like that, the cloud disappeared, and they were in clear air again. Jess pulled her arm back in and exclaimed, 'That was *amazing!*'

'It's one of my favourite things about flying up here,' he said, still facing the sky.

This had already been one of the most special experiences of her life. She reached out and touched his leg. He turned, and their eyes caught like a jagged fingernail on a thread of fabric. 'Thank you again. I will never forget this,' she said.

He held her gaze for a moment, his brown eyes thoughtful, before he gave a curt nod and turned to look outside again.

Jess took stock of herself. So far, this had been great, like nothing she'd done before. There was no problem with her stomach, and none of the nausea Gabriel had warned her about. Every vein in her body flowed with life. Up here, she felt invincible. She couldn't stop smiling.

'Versailles.' Gabriel pointed ahead.

In the distance, she noted a change in the landscape. Beyond a long, stone building, expansive squares of greenery took over. Broccoli trees squashed together with celery trees. Manicured gardens. Man-made water features.

Turning to her, he said, 'Things are going to get a bit more... dynamic, shall we say.'

'Dynamic?' Her happy haze fizzled. She didn't like the sound of this. It struck her as a euphemism for *dangerous*.

'Just know that it's perfectly safe. That's why we're both wearing 5-point harnesses. But I need Jacques to manoeuvre the helicopter so I can shoot straight down at the ground or else I won't be able to get the shot.'

'Straight down?' Her imagination caught up to his words. 'You mean...?'

'He'll be doing steep, banked circles over the spot I need. But like I said, we've done this many times before. You need to trust us, okay?'

Jess gulped and tried to recapture the brave part of herself, now slippery as an eel. She'd already climbed on the rollercoaster and was sitting on the ride, listening to the click-click-click as the cab rose higher and higher towards a steep drop. There was no escape. This was happening.

Panic arose, and her breathing sped up. She must remember to avoid all photographers in the future. They were all crazy in one way or another.

'Hey, hey,' said Gabriel, taking her trembling hand in his, forcing her to be still. 'You're going to be fine.'

He appeared so sincere, so utterly calm and composed beneath his head of hair blowing in the shifting wind. She allowed some of his serenity to seep into her. She nodded. 'I'm fine. Do what you have to do.'

With a wink he turned away, a sudden look of joy and anticipation on his face. He obviously loved this. He picked up his camera, ready to get his shot. Jess pressed herself back into her seat, her fingers weaving into her harness. She shut her eyes. She sensed the helicopter climbing higher by a change in the direction of air and the increased downward forces on her body.

Gabriel's deep, relaxed voice rolled into her ears like he was lecturing a class on aerial photography. 'On these trips, I'm looking to get a mix of shots. Some are close up, more abstract pictures of shapes and patterns I see on the ground. The others are oblique, three-quarter shots across the landscape.'

Gratitude seized her. She knew he was talking to keep her distracted.

Jacques said something and Gabriel replied, 'Ready or not, here we go.'

The helicopter sped up, and she tensed. The craft swung into a circular pattern, her body shifting more towards horizontal than vertical and straining against her harness as they banked steeply. She refused to open her eyes. Part of her prepared to scream, but she bit her tongue, not wanting to burst anyone's eardrums. Instead, she swore loudly. From Gabriel, she heard an exuberant *yee-hah*. He was more American than she thought. As the copter went round and round, the G-force pressed her back into her seat even as her braid flopped across her face towards the earth.

She understood what he meant about the nausea. It came on suddenly and fiercely as the helicopter rotated over its target. How could he even take pictures in this scenario? How could he keep calm enough to remember how to operate a camera?

And then, just as quickly as it started, it ended. Her braid settled. The force lessened. Only a ghost of the nausea lingered.

'You okay?' Gabriel asked as he scrolled through the images on the back of his camera like they hadn't been in a human centrifuge for the past minute.

All she could do was nod.

'If you need to vomit, let me know. I have some bags.'

What a gentleman. 'No.' Her brain performed a quick diagnostic of her stomach. 'I think I'm okay.'

For the next fifteen minutes, they alternated between getting wide landscape shots and targeting specific patterns on the ground. She appreciated the speed at which Jacques and Gabriel worked. Only once did Gabriel need to ask for a second twirly whirly, as she called them, because he hadn't gotten the right angle the first time.

On the third or fourth orbit (she lost count), Jess managed to crack one eye open. Gabriel was hanging as far out as the harness would let him, camera lens trained on the ground, his two-tone hair flapping in the wind like those inflatable air dancers outside car dealerships. She had to admire his bravery. She would be too scared to do that.

By the same token, she would have laughed if someone had told her earlier today she would be sitting in a helicopter above Versailles that evening. Yet here she was. Funny how quickly life could change. She wished she could send Krish a pic of what she was up to with a message, something like: 'I said yes to something else.'

This was definitely taking her mind off the fact that she was supposed to be getting a ring on her finger about now.

By the fifth orbit, she managed to keep her eyes wide open. By the sixth, she started to enjoy the view. They were spinning over the gardens closest to the big house when she noticed something cute about them. 'It's a face!' she said with excitement.

Indeed, the design of the landscaping below resembled a smiling cartoon bear, with two round algae-covered pools for eyes, a fountain in the middle of another oval pool for a nose, and a happy smile made out of shrubbery. Jess laughed. When they settled again, Gabriel nudged her with his elbow and showed her the images on the back of his camera.

'Wow,' she said. What more could she say? The man was talented. 'What do you do with the people in the photo? Do you just…?' She made an erasing motion with her finger.

'Sometimes, but not always. I think they give a sense of scale.'

'And the shadows?' She noticed the black, tooth-like shapes on the ground to the left of some shrubs, reminding her of spikes on a collar. 'Is that why you schedule these shoots at the end of the day?

So the shadows are more interesting?' She hadn't dated a photographer for two years and learnt nothing.

'Exactly!' he said with enthusiasm. 'If I'm shooting for colour, like shorelines where I'm creating more abstract work, then I'll shoot late morning or early afternoon. But for cities, sunrise or sunset is best. The shadows help to give it a more 3D effect. More visual interest.' She had to smile at how earnest he looked while explaining this all to her, his face open and animated—a distant stranger to the serious man she'd met earlier.

She realised that he loved what he did. It made her feel a connection to him. She loved teaching, too. It didn't gift her a lot of *yee-hah* moments, but she found it satisfying. That look on her children's faces when they were discovering something new gave her all the feels.

He touched her on the hand and her eyes snapped to his face. He leaned towards her and pointed through the front of the helicopter. 'Look at Versailles.'

Jess turned her head to observe the long baroque building, covered in windows like keys on a piano.

Gabriel continued, 'See how the light is hitting it?'

'It's glowing,' she said with wonder. The beige stone blushed orange in the diminishing sunshine, and light bounced off the glass, making the whole edifice pop out from the landscape. The helicopter swung around and hovered, so that Gabriel could shoot the gardens with the massive building at the top. Jess peered over his shoulder. The beauty of the vista made her gasp, and the sight imprinted itself on her memory. For a moment, emotion overcame her, and she choked on a silent sob.

How lucky was she to be seeing Versailles from this angle, high above the earth, high above the people in the gardens? The bodies down there might be from any era: that one could be Marie Antoinette;

another one could be a mother pushing a pram while reading her phone; still another could be a projection of Jess as a tourist tomorrow. Past, present or future. It could all be going on at the same time down there, but she hovered above, one of them, but not one of them. Out of time and space. A strong sense of being separate from everyday life, but at the same time connected intimately to the earth flowed through her.

That building down there oversaw hundreds of years of history, seen millions of people, each with their own worries, concerns, hopes and dreams.

Like a switch flipping, Jess knew that she would survive. Krish had left her. So what? In the grand scheme of things, it didn't matter. Jess would go on. Life would go on. The earth would go on.

This was her tiny little story, and it was up to her to make it a happy one.

Maybe he'd done her a favour. Maybe they were just never meant to be.

A tear slipped from her eye and blew away in the wind.

The helicopter jerked out of its hover, snapping Jess from her trance. She shook her head and touched her hand to her temple. *What the heck was that?* Last year, she remembered researching some new space facts to share with her class, when she came across something called 'The Overview Effect'—a term coined to describe something experienced by astronauts when they gazed at the earth from space: a transformative experience triggered by an extraordinary visual stimulus resulting in feelings of deep connection to the planet, awe, self-transcendence, and sometimes a shift in values. She wondered if she'd just experienced a version of that.

'You all right?' asked Gabriel, touching her leg with concern.

Their eyes connected, and she felt the urge to kiss him again— just to say thank you for caring. But remembering last time, she fought it. Instead she said, 'I'm more than alright. I'm amazing.' She smiled. She would have whooped if she didn't think it would be too loud in their headphones.

Gabriel narrowed his gaze and said, 'You want to whoop, don't you?'

'How did you know?' It was like he'd read her mind

He shrugged. 'It's natural, especially your first time. So...go ahead. Do it.'

'Really?'

'I'll whoop with you. Ready? One...two...three...'

And they both let loose, her higher voice and his lower one, hooting together like children. She saw Jacques shaking his head. Both Gabriel and she dissolved into laughter at the end. She wiped moisture from her eyes, as the helicopter swung around for another shot and he got back to work.

Too soon, their forty-five minutes were up, and they began their return journey to the heliport.

'Did you get everything you wanted?' Jess asked.

'And more,' he said, his eyes dropping to her lips. Her stomach did an unexpected flip.

The sun descended over the horizon and tungsten lights peppered the darkening Parisian cityscape. The air lashing through the cabin turned chillier and, in a moment of daring, she pressed her right side closer to the man next to her, sucking in his warmth, enjoying the animal pleasure of his body connected to hers. In a moment of further daring, she let her head rest on his shoulder. After sharing this experience with Gabriel, she felt close to him in a way that transcended the physical.

'Thank you for this,' she said into the mic again.

She threaded her fingers through his. At first, she felt him pull away, but then he seemed to change his mind, letting her hold his hand.

This evening had been perfect. And it wasn't over yet.

6

GABRIEL KNEW WHEN A WOMAN WANTED TO HAVE SEX WITH HIM.

Call it a sixth sense. Call it whatever. Right now, Jess was sending out some pretty strong signals. As the taxi raced back to Montmartre, she sat to his left on the back seat, her leg pressing into his. She still held his hand, their fingers interlaced. Both gazed out opposite windows, but the air was thick with tension. He caught himself more than once running his thumb up and down her knuckles. He stopped himself each time.

He hadn't decided yet whether this would be a good idea or not.

Sex for Gabriel was both complicated and uncomplicated at the same time. Uncomplicated because he never allowed sex to mean anything more than the physical act. A way to gain release. No emotions. No long-term relationships. As soon as he felt that a partner wanted more than he could give, he'd break things off.

It had been six months since the last time he'd slept with someone. He barely remembered her name. Sara? Sylvie? She had been an art buyer from a corporate interiors company in Lausanne. His agent had insisted that he take the woman to dinner because she was placing a big order for his work. It had been a pleasant night: dinner

47

with interesting conversation, followed by a mutual, adult decision to take things further. The next morning, she left and he hadn't heard from her since—just how he liked it.

On the other hand, sex was complicated for him. Every time he got physical with a new woman and she saw the effects of war on his body, it meant she would want to have certain conversations— conversations that he might find hard to have, especially right now.

And a couple of times, women had taken one look and walked away. His thoughts returned to a hotel room in Rome, after he completed an aerial advertising job. He'd met her in the bar, a banker from New York. He could still see the shocked expression on her face when he undressed for her. She left fast. Some women couldn't handle his baggage, he guessed.

He didn't think Jess would do that. At least, he hoped she wouldn't.

Gabriel sighed and flicked his eyes towards his right leg. Had she noticed anything? He realised he was stroking her thumb again and stopped.

What to do?

Something was holding him back. He couldn't put his finger on it, but he got the feeling that Jess might be dangerous to the fragile web of control he'd built around himself. He'd already found himself acting rashly, inviting her on his ride to Versailles.

It had been worth it, though. He had just watched this woman bloom before his eyes, going from scared to intrigued to excited. A ride like that changed a person—he knew this first-hand. After his recovery, he hadn't wanted to touch his camera again. That small black box that had once meant so much to him, even obsessed him, now held too many complicated memories. Then, a photographer friend in Australia had invited Gabriel up in a helicopter to try aerial photography…and he was hooked. In some ways, that trip had probably saved his life. It definitely gave him a new perspective and something to live for. When he was in the air, he felt like himself again.

Tonight, he had observed Jess, in between taking his photos (which were awesome, by the way). She had gone into that helicopter one person and come out another. He knew that her body was currently full of adrenaline, that life was coursing through her... because that's how he'd felt the first time. Completely alive after feeling dead.

And it had the added effect of making a person horny as hell.

He shifted uncomfortably. One part of his body was already placing its vote. He hoped she hadn't noticed the bulge in his jeans.

Should he risk it? One part of him argued that she would only be in town for a handful of days. For her, it would be a holiday romance, a way to get over her heartbreak. For him, it would be the desperately needed sexual top-up that his body craved. No danger of her forming an attachment to him, of needing him for anything beyond a body to enjoy.

As far as situations went, it couldn't get more ideal than this. And he couldn't deny his attraction to her. She had a mouth that begged to be kissed.

He just wished the insecure voice at the back of his head would shut up, the one that always said: what if she took one look at him and ran?

THE TAXI DOOR SLAMMED, and Jess waited in front of the apartment building as Gabriel heaved his bag out of the car boot.

She drank in the night.

Montmartre came alive in the dark. Groups of tourists wandered by, searching for magic in the place that Picasso, Monet, Renoir, and Toulouse-Lautrec called home. The restaurants spilled over with customers; the hubbub of conversation and people enjoying each other's company filled the air. Glasses tinkled as they clinked together. Music from a nearby busker curled around her—songs of love sung in a husky French voice.

Every nerve ending in her body tingled, and she couldn't wipe the contented smile off of her face. Energy zinged through her. Something about being above the earth and seeing it from a new vantage point made her feel closer to it. And touching the cloud... she'd never forget that moment as long as she lived.

Jess glanced towards the restaurant where she'd gotten pissed last night. She spied the same waiter working the tables. She turned her back before he clocked her.

Gabriel joined her in front of the door. He ran a hand through his hair and dipped his head towards the ground as though he was thinking about something. With a sigh, he dropped his arm and said, 'So, do you want to come up for dinner? I'm sure I can rustle something up for us.' His frown had returned. Was it just her or did he seem nervous? Surely not. The Gabriel she knew had been the picture of self-confidence since she'd met him.

'Yeah, that would be great.' Did he really mean dinner...or was he talking about something else?

He held open the front door for her. As they waited for the lift, she was aware of him standing behind her—not close enough to touch, just close enough to make the back of her neck go prickly.

She wanted sex. Unadulterated, passionate, skin-on-skin, licking, sucking sex. She glanced over her shoulder and smiled at him shyly, at first. Why was she being coy about what she wanted? *Let him see that you desire him*, she thought. Taking a deep breath, Jess wiped the shyness from her smile and dipped hungry eyes to his mouth, taking her bottom lip between her teeth. From the way Gabriel watched her every move with his intense, hooded eyes, she suspected he had a similar desire.

An anticipatory warmth ignited between her legs as they entered the four-person lift. She sensed the presence of his body in the tight space as though he was pushed right up against her, when in reality a camera bag kept them apart. Seized by another burst of timidity, she studied her trainers, aware that he was watching her in the mirrored walls of the lift. Could she really do it? This would be another first for her. Sex to her had always meant love and commitment. She never slept with a man until she was certain of both their feelings. She'd made Krish wait two months.

But she was Yes Jess now. And after that flight, she wanted Gabriel in a 100% physical, animalistic way that was completely new to her. Two consenting adults…consenting.

The lift opened and she realised that he lived on the top floor. The penthouse.

As he punched in the code to unlock the door to his flat, she ran her fingers over her lips and studied how his hair curled at the back of his neck. She wondered what his hair would smell like up close and involuntarily leaned towards him while breathing in deeply. Sweet and musky. *Some species of bats use the sense of smell to find a mate with the greatest genetic diversity*, she thought out of the blue. Useless fact no 368.

If it worked for bats, then it would work for her.

She leaned back again before he caught her sniffing him like a lunatic.

His door opened and she followed him in. Gabriel flicked the lights on and she stopped in her tracks. For a moment, she had the same sense of déjà vu that she'd had earlier in his gallery. The world fuzzed and then realigned, leaving her with a slight wooziness. She shook her head to dispel the sensation.

Jess didn't know what she'd been expecting his personal space to look like, but not this. For one, she thought he'd have loads of photographs on his walls, but there were none. Instead, his apartment was like a greenhouse, full of vibrant houseplants with a huge bank of windows facing the street and curving towards the ceiling— much bigger than her studio downstairs. It was mostly open-plan, with some more rooms on the other side of the kitchen and stairs leading up to a mezzanine. He had shelves that stretched across most of the far wall, packed with books and more of those gold-veined ceramics like the ones in her place.

'What are these?' she asked, walking to the shelves and leaning over to examine a delicate white vase criss-crossed with fissures.

'It's called *Kintsugi*—literally *golden repair* in Japanese. The art of being broken.' Gabriel released his camera bag onto the kitchen island and took off his leather jacket, laying it on top.

'It's stunning.' She ran her finger along the metallic seam, marvelling at how the scars elevated the ceramic's appeal, making them something new. Maybe she could repair Pierre this way.

He crossed the room to stand next to her and picked up one of the pieces, a cobalt blue bowl webbed with gold lines. 'I do it to help me meditate. I find it relaxing.'

As her hip brushed his, she felt anything but relaxed. Jess swallowed and asked, 'Do you break them yourself or...?'

'Sometimes. I visit secondhand shops, flea markets...Paris has a lot of them.' He put the bowl back down on the shelf.

'I *love* flea markets,' said Jess. 'You never know what you're going to find.' A little bit like wandering into galleries off the street...

She bit her lip. Through his tight/not-tight linen shirt, she discerned the shape of his torso: strong and trim. Her fingers itched to touch him, but the thought of making the first move terrified her. What if he rebuffed her again, like last night? What if this longing was one-sided?

Their eyes snagged and held. 'There's something poetic about finding something broken and making it stronger, more beautiful...' He reached out to tuck a tendril of hair behind her ear.

In that moment, she understood what they were: two broken people finding strength in each other.

Maybe he was her golden glue.

She decided to take a leap. Closing her eyes, she tilted her head, leaned in, and waited.

Hot breath feathered across her cheek as he stepped closer, their bodies almost touching. One of his hands slid under her hair and cradled her neck. She pressed into it, craving the connection with him. His thumb wiped across her bottom lip and she shivered. Instinctually, she took his thumb into her mouth and sucked. He inhaled sharply.

She released his thumb. 'Gabriel,' she whispered without opening her eyes.

In response, he leaned in, took her bottom lip lightly between his teeth, and ran his tongue along the edge. The ache in her breasts and between her legs intensified. This slow journey towards a kiss was sweet torture. Maybe there was something to this idea that French men made the best lovers.

He released her lip and, for a second, she hung in space, in suspense waiting for his next touch. She kept her eyes firmly closed, not wanting to ruin the surprise.

A butterfly kiss landed near the spot just below her ear. At the same time, the hand not cradling her head slipped under her shirt and caressed the naked skin of her waist, raising goosebumps all over her body.

Her entire being ached from the fire he was stoking in her.

His lips moved across her jaw and returned to her mouth.

Pulling away for a moment, he said, 'Just to be clear, I'm not looking for anything serious. This is just—'

'*Sex*,' Jess confirmed as she took his head between her hands and pulled him forcefully to her. Her tongue darted into his mouth a little, then back again, then a little bit more, until their tongues lashed against each other in a hungry dance. He tasted of the hard ginger candies they'd both been sucking after the flight. Tangy and delicious. *So this is what French kissing should be like,* she thought. Not that she hadn't kissed with tongues before. She had, plenty of times. But usually it took a little while to get used to someone else's unique style. Gabriel suited her perfectly from the beginning.

Her hands slid from his face, down his neck, and settled on his chest. At the same time he pulled her closer to him and she felt his need for her pressing against her, further enflaming her. 'Gabriel,' she whispered, loving how the three syllables of his name slid past her lips.

Something about making out with a semi-stranger made it even hotter. No expectations. No plans for tomorrow. Just pleasure and sensation. Enjoying the beauty of connection without possession.

His lips left hers and nibbled their way to her ear and neck. She groaned. Pulling away for a moment, she hastily took off her hoody and threw it on the floor before entering his arms again. She wanted to feel his hands on her breasts without unnecessary layers between them.

Gabriel did not disappoint. As their lips found each other again, he moved his hand up under her shirt, his thumb grazing the bottom of her breast. Thank goodness she had brought her best lingerie for her trip. She'd read somewhere that French men got off on sexy bras and pants.

'Is this all right with you?' he asked, and she nodded enthusiastically. Delicious, wicked hunger surged through her. She wanted him so badly. She could barely breath through the need that gripped her entire body.

So when his kisses slowed and he pushed her away a few inches, disappointment made her stammer, 'I-I thought...'

Before she could say any more, he stopped her. 'I want you. But...I just need to do something first. Will you wait here?'

'Yeah...sure.'

He kissed her quickly on the lips and then disappeared into a room on the other side of the kitchen. Presumably his bedroom.

Across the room, she caught sight of herself in a mirror hanging on the wall. Even though her hair was still in a plait, curls sprang loose everywhere, giving her a wild look. Her lips were swollen and red from kissing, and her eyes sparkled with desire. Who was this temptress? She barely recognised the sensual woman staring back at her.

The sound of cupboard doors opening and closing and bed springs groaning pulled her out of her self-examination.

What was he doing in there? Was he tidying up, like Laura Linney in her favourite Christmas movie, *Love, Actually*? Or maybe he was putting on a gimp suit! Suddenly she realised that she didn't really know him at all. And nobody knew where she was. He could be a crazed killer. She didn't get that vibe, but that didn't mean it wasn't possible. Psychopaths tended to be charming.

Maybe it was a good thing that he'd put the brakes on things. She didn't want to do something she'd regret tomorrow. Maybe she'd had enough spontaneity for one day with their helicopter trip.

That being said, her body still hummed with desire.

He re-entered the room. He had changed into a pair of shorts and it didn't take her long to see why.

He wore a lower-limb prosthetic on his right leg.

Gabriel was an amputee.

How had she not noticed it before? She played through the past day trying to identify a point where she might have suspected, but couldn't single out anything. As a teacher *and* a Virgo, being observant was usually one of her superpowers. Then again, she hadn't noticed her ex-boyfriend falling out of love with her, so...

'Hey,' he said as he stopped in front of her.

'I-I didn't know,' she said, feeling stupid for being so blind. So many thoughts and questions jumbled through her head. How had it happened? How had he survived it? Did it still hurt him?

'I'm pretty good at hiding it from people,' he said. 'But I didn't want it to come as a surprise when...when we...'

She stepped towards him and placed a finger on his lips. 'Shhh. I understand.' And she did. She appreciated that he thought to tell her before things went further. She wondered if he'd had a bad sexual experience in the past with someone who'd reacted poorly. Silently, she cursed any woman who had ever made him feel less because of this.

'Do you still want to...?' His eyes grew wary and moved to her ear as though meeting her gaze was too difficult.

Jess saw a new side to Gabriel. Less confident. Vulnerable. More real than the whooping hotshot she'd seen in the helicopter and more accessible than the grumpy gallery owner. 'I do, but...maybe not all the way? It's not because of your leg,' she rushed to reassure him. 'It's because of me. I was already having second thoughts while you were in your room. I'm not usually a spontaneous sex kind of girl.'

His dark eyes moved back to hers, and it was her turn to drop her gaze. 'Why not?'

'Why not what?' She shrugged.

'Why aren't you a spontaneous sex kind of girl? Sex is natural. And you're beautiful.' He took the end of her plait in his fingers and slid the elastic off of the end. Slowly, he unbraided it.

She shook out her curls to hide her blush at his compliment. 'I don't know. Just the way...the way I was raised, I guess. All the books I read when I was a young girl, they made it seem like sleeping with men without a relationship was, you know, *slutty*, and I sort of took that message to heart.'

'Well, it's not slutty. The French don't think so, anyway.' He pulled her into his arms and leaned over to kiss her jaw. 'I'm happy to be led by you. There are many'—kiss—'*many* ways I can give you pleasure that don't involve full sex.' His mouth moved to her ear and he nibbled the lobe, making her shiver.

If that wasn't the hottest thing a man had ever said to her, she didn't know what was. His words darted straight to her core, and a myriad of ideas and exciting possibilities blossomed in her imagination. Things she'd never done before, too embarrassed or too prudish to let herself be exposed. But for some reason, Gabriel made her feel it was okay to be adventurous. It seemed natural with him.

Right now, she wanted Gabriel to show her what she'd been missing. 'Let's go to your bedroom,' she whispered.

Taking her hand, he led the way.

7

THE FOLLOWING MORNING, JESS WOKE UP FIRST. JUST ENOUGH LIGHT seeped around the stone-coloured curtains for her to make out the man lying next to her, flat on his back and fast asleep.

She pushed herself up on her elbows. His right leg lay on top of the duvet, ending around halfway down his calf. He had excused himself to remove his prosthesis and wash his stump after their first round of orgasms. She was glad when he'd done it because, although he did his best to keep it away from her, the few times her skin brushed past it had felt strange: cold and metallic. She preferred him without it—at least in bed.

Studying his muscular thigh, she swept her eyes down over the scarred, rounded end of his leg. The skin was puckered and red, alternating between smooth and rough. She could see two lines where the doctors must have sutured it closed. The urge to run her fingers over those lines forced its way into her mind; she squeezed her hand into a fist, knowing without being told how intimate that would be—even more intimate than what they'd done last night. Worried that he might not like it if he woke up and found her staring at his leg, she moved her gaze to his face.

In the dim light, she observed the dark stubble on his jaw, the one that she had kissed many times last night and the same jaw that had rubbed against the inside of her leg as he licked her into oblivion.

A huge grin spread across her face, which she immediately covered with her hand. The things they did last night...

Her audacity made her want to laugh and hide at the same time.

With a languid stretch, she laid back down and closed her eyes. Her hand stroked the skin around her belly button as she relived some of the more exhilarating moments from the previous evening's sexy time olympics. She had never felt so free with previous partners. Gabriel had brought her to orgasm multiple times in different ways: with his fingers, with his tongue, from the front, from the back. He had explored parts of her that she'd never previously allowed anyone to touch.

Yes, she meant *there*. That had been an unexpected delight.

This spontaneity science fair project, as Gabriel called it, was really working out for her.

In fact, she might never want to go back to penetrative sex ever again, now that she knew so much more about the other stuff. That being said, part of her regretted that she'd set limits on what she'd do with him last night. He was obviously a master, and she wondered what the full act would have been like with him. It made her want to have another go...

Sighing, she rolled over and picked up the glass on her bedside table. Last night had been thirsty work. As she sipped the water, her eyes fell on a framed photograph on top of the fireplace mantel. In it was a younger Gabriel, his hair more black than grey, wearing comfortable beige clothing like the type of outfit a person would wear in a desert. A leanly-muscled, dark-haired woman in a khaki green vest top hugged him, and he hugged her back. Their heads faced different directions, but both were laughing. Jess was surprised at the irrational frisson of jealousy she felt.

'*Bonjour*,' said Gabriel behind her. He ran a finger lightly down the middle of her back and a quiver ran through her.

'Morning.' She flipped onto her other side, so that she faced him, her smile both shy and wicked at the same time.

'Sleep all right?' His hair was sticking up on one side, and he was so adorable and mussed, she longed to touch it and flatten it down, but ignored the urge. She didn't know him well enough, which was a funny notion considering what they'd done last night.

Instead, she bit her lip and nodded. 'You?'

'Surprisingly well.'

There were so many questions she wanted to ask him, but it was probably a bit rude to launch into them straight after waking up. At the very least, she should let him have some coffee first.

He reached out and pulled her towards him. Jess cuddled into his side, her head resting on his shoulder and her fingers playing with the wiry hairs on his chest. She inhaled the faint residue of his cologne overlayed with the pleasantly sour-sweet scent of good sex.

Gabriel sighed. 'Go ahead.'

'What?' She angled her head to look at his profile.

'Ask your questions. I can tell you're dying to know.'

She dropped her head onto his shoulder again. 'Am I that transparent?'

He just laughed. 'Yes.'

'Okay. Well.' She didn't want to start at the deep end, so she back-tracked to the beginning. 'When did you first realise you wanted to photograph war zones? I mean, how do you even get started in that kind of career?' The idea of choosing to put oneself in danger for a living completely boggled her mind. As a primary school teacher in England, the biggest danger she encountered were over-sharpened pencils.

With a sharp huff, he said, 'By being the perfect combination of idealistic, young, and stupid. When we lived in New Jersey, I went to a top boy's school. Think *Dead Poet's Society* but without the boarding. Anyway, they taught us that we were kings of the world, future captains of industry. Invincible. I believed them.

'And then, before my senior year, I met a boy from Rwanda at soccer camp. He told me about the genocide in his country...both his parents had been killed and he and his sister were living with an aunt and uncle in the US...and I just thought, *how did I not know about this?* I'd been living in a safe bubble, completely oblivious. I couldn't stop thinking about what I had been doing when all those people were being massacred. That was the beginning for me. I wanted to show others what was going on in the world because if they saw, then they'd care, right?' He laughed without humour. 'I wanted to understand war, the mechanics of it. How it affected people. I wanted to watch history happening and then once I started doing it —it was like a drug. The more dangerous, the better. I was always the last to leave when a situation got risky. I thought I was indestructible.'

Glancing down towards his stump, she finally asked, 'How did you lose your foot?'

A few beats passed before he exhaled and said quickly, as though trying to get the words out of his mouth as fast as possible, 'We were taken hostage in the mountains of Afghanistan. *This*' —he gestured downwards—'happened just before the US Army turned up to free us.'

Jess stayed silent. She detected that there was more, and she wanted to give him the safe space to say it. 'Our kidnappers shot me in the foot. Or, more accurately, they shot off my foot. By the time the soldiers got me to the hospital, they were worried about infection. So they amputated halfway up my calf. I don't remember it.'

Her eyes swelled with tears. She couldn't even imagine the agony, the loneliness and the fear he must have experienced, so far away from home and the people who loved him. Her heart expanded to three times its natural size with feeling for him. She wanted to take him in her arms and kiss away his pain.

Seeking to give him comfort, she turned her face up and leaned towards his cheek. He jerked his head in the other direction, and his whole body tensed up.

Seconds as long as an eternity passed before he relaxed. 'Sorry.' He sat up, pulling his arm out from under her. Sitting on the edge of the bed, fully naked, he said, 'I don't talk about it much. It was eight years ago.' He tugged on a drawer in his bedside table and retrieved a flesh-coloured silicon sock.

Jess felt stupid. While his back was to her, she wiped at her eyes and willed the rest of her tears back into her head. She sat up against the padded headboard, pulling the duvet up to cover herself, already mourning the closeness they'd shared only moments ago. 'No, I'm sorry I pried. It's your story to tell or not tell. I mean, who am I? I'm nobody to you.'

Gabriel stopped what he was doing and pinned her with his honest gaze. 'That's not true. You're somebody.'

They stared at each other as the room brightened a bit more, the sun coming out from behind a cloud outside.

The moment passed, and Gabriel turned his attention to the rubbery sock in his hand. He placed the closed end against his stump and rolled it up, similar to donning a condom.

Jess thought about the picture on the mantelpiece. The next question hung on her lips, daring her to ask it: *'Who's the woman in the photo?'* But she didn't. She suspected that this woman had been purposefully left out of the story. If he'd wanted to tell her, he would have. He wasn't Jess's boyfriend, and he didn't owe her explanations for anything.

The sound of the front door opening made Gabriel whip around.

'Bonjour!' called a female voice. She said something else in French.

'Merde,' said Gabriel.

A sick feeling squirmed in Jess's stomach, and she sat forward in the bed like a meerkat. Was it his girlfriend? The woman in the picture? Had Jess just slept with a taken man? Was she about to have the Frenchest of French experiences: being discovered in someone else's lover's bed?

Gabriel saw the horrified look on her face and said, 'No, no. Don't worry. It's my well-intentioned, but annoying sister.' He reached across to a bureau of drawers, conveniently placed within arm's reach for him, and took out a pair of black tracksuit bottoms.

Relief flooded through Jess. The other woman scenario was *not* on her bucket list. She immediately thought back to the day she'd arrived and the friendly, petite woman with the brown pony tail and Audrey Hepburn vibes who greeted her.

He shouted something out in French and, to Jess, said in a low voice, 'Stay in here if you want.' Shimmying the right leg of the tracksuit over his prosthetic, which already had his shoe attached to the end, he slid his stump into the plastic socket at the top, then rolled another flesh-coloured sock up to cover the first one.

Was he ashamed of having Jess in his bed? She hugged the duvet to her body self-consciously, even as she watched the myriad of tiny adjustments he had to make to accommodate his missing limb. 'Do... do you want me to stay in here?'

Gabriel raised his eyebrows, stuck out his lower lip, and shrugged in a very Gallic way. She interpreted it as saying *I don't care*, which made her feel sad, like she didn't matter to him. 'It's up to you.' He tied the matching shoe onto his other foot.

He stood with his back to her, delicately testing his balance on his prosthesis, and then shrugged into a black t-shirt. Making his way to the door with his usual confident stride, he said, 'I'll go out and meet her. Take your time.'

Gabriel left. Jess flopped back on the bed, staring at the ceiling. *'Take your time'*...it sounded like something a waiter might say after you'd paid your bill, when he wanted you to leave, but also didn't want to rush you in case you left a bad tip.

And thus endeth my French Fling, she thought. While he put on his prosthetic and dressed himself, she detected the old Gabriel returning piece by piece—the furrowed brow, the hard stare, the clenched jaw. Gone was the more sensitive man she'd been with last night, replaced by his irritable twin.

More tears gathered behind her eyes, now for a different reason. Despite the short time she'd know him, a connection had formed between them, at least on her side. They had shared something special, not just in bed, but also in the helicopter. Last night had mattered to her, even if she was just another conquest for him.

Perhaps she wasn't cut out to be a spontaneous sex kind of girl, after all.

Wiping the tears away from her eyes and taking a deep breath, she flung off the covers and gathered her clothes. In the other room, she heard Gabriel and Elodie talking together. His everyday life was going on in that kitchen, and Jess felt like an intruder.

She thrust her legs into her jeans, put on her t-shirt, and went into his en-suite bathroom to brush her teeth. In the middle of the night, he had given her the code to his front door, so she could sneak back to her flat and get her toothbrush and toothpaste. As much as she had enjoyed being spontaneous, she drew the line at not brushing her teeth. Her dad was a dentist, after all.

Dropping her supplies into her bag, she slung it over her shoulder before carefully making the bed. She committed to memory his dark green walls, the patterned rug, the triangular motif on his neutral duvet, tucking away mental snapshots for a rainy day. Before she left, she picked up the picture of him with the woman and took a closer look. She could see now that they both had camera straps looped around their necks. Both had white patches around their eyes to mark where their sunglasses usually sat. She squinted at his eyebrow. No scar. Behind them, dry, rocky terrain filled the background. It looked like Afghanistan, Libya, Iraq, the Grand Canyon or about a hundred other places.

The grinding noise of a coffee machine encroached on her thoughts, and Jess put the picture back where she'd found it. After smoothing her hands down the front of her jeans with a long exhale, she pasted a smile on her face and left the refuge of his room.

In the kitchen, Elodie was sitting at the dining table, drinking a foaming cup of coffee. Assorted pastries were piled high on a plate in front of her. Jess admired her outfit: a bright green, sleeveless sundress with a white Peter Pan collar and a matching hairband. Simple and chic.

Elodie stopped in the middle of saying something, switching to the same perfect American accent as Gabriel: 'Well, hello there.' Belying her youthful, Sunday-school ready appearance, the corners of her lips turned up like a Cheshire Cat looking forward to a bowl of cream, and a devilish gleam glinted in her wide, Disney princess eyes.

'Hi...again,' said Jess, knowing that her cheeks had gone bright red.

'I must say, this is a delightful surprise.' Elodie threw her brother a pointed look.

He grunted in response.

Jess tilted her head. When she'd first met Elodie, she had clearly spoken English with a French accent. Reading her confusion, Elodie said, 'The accent, right? I always speak with a French one when I'm meeting the guests. I feel that if I turned up sounding like a cast member from *Friends*, it would sort of ruin the romantic tourist experience. But now, you know. Don't reveal my secret in your review, please.'

'Oh. Of course not.' Nodding, Jess cast about for something else to say, but came up empty-handed. This was so awkward.

Elodie had no such problems. She made a bridge with her hands and propped her chin coquettishly on top. 'Speaking of secrets, how did you two meet?'

Jess looked at Gabriel for help, and their eyes met. A flashback of his face bathed with passion flickered through her mind, and heat flared inside her again.

'Er...' said Jess. What had Elodie asked?

'None of your business.' He glared at his sister. 'Coffee?' he asked Jess.

'Um, yes, please.'

Elodie patted the chair next to her, and Jess reluctantly sat down.

'So,' the delighted sister leaned in, 'are you enjoying your time in Paris?'

'Yes, it's been great so far.' *Because your brother is a sex demon*, she thought, colouring further.

Wiping the remaining foam off the inside of her mug with her index finger, Elodie asked, 'So what's your story? Tell me all about yourself.' She plopped her finger in her mouth and opened her eyes wide with interest. In the background, the coffee machine groaned as it spit out more liquid.

Where to begin? 'Well, I teach primary school in London—'

'No way!' Elodie seized Jess's arm with the speed of a ninja. 'Me too! What grade?'

Translating 'grade' into British English, Jess said, 'Year one...so that's five-year-olds.' She had to raise her voice to compete with the loud whoosh of pressurised air from the milk frother.

Grabbing a pastry and sitting back again, Elodie said, 'I teach fourth grade at an American School here in Paris.'

At Jess's confused look, Elodie clarified, 'Nine-year-olds.'

Gabriel placed a wide white mug full of cappuccino in front of Jess and took a seat across from them. 'You're a teacher?' He tore into a *pain au chocolat*.

'I can't believe I haven't told you that,' said Jess. It reminded her that he was still technically a stranger.

Elodie snorted and said, 'It's hard to talk when your mouth is full.'

Gabriel tossed his remaining croissant at her head and rebuked her in French. Elodie replied with something short and sharp and stroked her jawline twice with her knuckles in some sort of Gallic gesture. In return, he threw his hands in the air. Jess wished the floor would open up and swallow her. In the five minutes she'd been around this brother and sister duo, they'd argued more than her parents had in the twenty-eight years since she'd been born.

'Sorry,' Gabriel said, his expression resigned. 'My sister is an interfering busybody with no filter between her head and her mouth.'

'And my brother is a sad, boring hermit, so thank you for sleeping with him,' said Elodie. 'Seriously, you've done a great service to humanity.'

Jess's eyes bugged wide, and she didn't know where to look. The French were way less repressed about discussing sex openly. She seriously contemplated grabbing her bag and running away. A foot tapped against hers under the table, and she immediately knew it was Gabriel. Her eyes found his. With his usual dry-humour, he explained. 'Sorry, she isn't very well trained.' To Elodie: 'I can't believe you're responsible for teaching children.'

She snapped her tongue dismissively and said, 'Whatever. Anyway, what are you two doing today?'

'Um...I have no plans,' said Jess, assuming that Gabriel might not want to spend more time with her, but by the same token, leaving herself open to an invitation.

Gabriel's smile dropped, his expression turning almost angry and his eyes darkening. To his sister, he said, 'You *know* what I'm doing today.'

JULIA BOGGIO

She actually winced and looked contrite for the first time. 'Shit, sorry, G. I forgot...' The mood shifted, and Jess couldn't follow what was happening. All she knew was that she was back to feeling like an interloper again.

Not wanting to outstay her welcome, Jess pushed away from the table and stood up. She refused to be that last guest at the party who didn't know when it was time to leave. 'It's okay. I think I'm going to just walk around today.'

'Nope,' said Elodie, standing to join her. 'You're coming with me. It's the summer picnic at my school.'

'Oh, I couldn't—'

'Please! It will be about a trillion times more fun with you there. Free food...' She sang it as though free food might be the best reason to do anything, and Jess hailed from the workhouse in *Oliver Twist*.

'Um...' Jess wasn't sure. She didn't know Elodie, and she didn't want Gabriel to think she was expecting anything from him or schmoozing with his sister to crawl deeper into his life. Jess hadn't read the rule book for one-night stands, but hanging out with the sister of the guy you'd slept with probably wasn't a recommended move.

Gabriel recovered from his dark cloud. He stood and gathered their empty mugs. 'What about your spontaneity science fair project?' He said it over his shoulder as he carried the items to the sink—both a challenge and permission for her to accept his sister's invitation.

She pursed her lips to the side. What could it hurt? She didn't know Paris at all, and it would be interesting to see what the American School looked like. Call it professional curiosity.

With a smile, she shrugged and said, 'Okay. I guess so. Why not?'

Elodie shrieked and did a funny dance. When she recovered, Elodie suggested they meet in front of the building in thirty minutes'

68

time. She excused herself and went to the toilet—Jess assumed, to give her and Gabriel a chance to say goodbye.

Picking up her bag, Jess strolled to the door. Gabriel stood at the sink, busily washing out mugs and lost in thought. He didn't seem to notice that she was leaving.

Unsure what to say, she cleared her throat. 'Um. So…I guess I'll see you around?' She didn't want to make any assumptions about whether he wanted to get together again before she left on Thursday. He didn't reply. 'Gabriel?'

His head snapped up and, for a fleeting moment, she caught the tail end of a helpless, ravaged expression on his face. Whatever he had going through his mind, it wasn't future assignations with Jess.

She dug her nails into her palm to stop herself from rushing over to comfort him. Although he appeared like he could use a hug, his manner conveyed it wouldn't be welcome. He turned off the tap and came towards her, stuffing his hands into his pockets—as though he wanted to avoid touching her.

Taking her cue from him, she wrapped her hands around her bag's strap. 'I guess this is it,' she said, wanting to set the bar first: no expectations.

He removed his hands from his pockets and crossed his arms instead. 'I'm pretty busy over the next few days—'

'Oh, of course, you are. I mean, why wouldn't you be?' She forced the corners of her lips to stay pointing up and avoided his eyes. 'Don't worry about me. There's plenty to—'

'If I find some free time, I'll call you. I've got your number on your booking.'

All Jess heard was, *Don't call us, we'll call you.* Never a positive sign. 'Great. Um. Sure. Well…bye!'

Before he noticed the moisture gathering in her lashes, she opened the door and headed directly to the lift. A very large part of her wanted him to come after her, to take her in his arms and kiss her one last time.

But he didn't.

As she stepped into the lift and pressed the button for her floor, a bitter laugh escaped her lips. On the bright side, she hadn't thought about Krish since yesterday.

8

For the first part of the journey on the Metro, Elodie quizzed Jess about herself, wanting to know where she was from, did she have brothers and sisters, what teacher training was like in the UK, who her parents were, what they did for a living...the questions were endless.

As they switched onto a bus at the Gare St Lazare, Elodie asked, 'So what's this stuff about a spontaneity science fair project?'

'Oh, it's nothing.' Jess blushed, embarrassed. Telling people that she'd just been dumped made her worry that the first thing they'd wonder was: *'What's wrong with her that he dumped her?'* Silly, she knew, but she couldn't help how she felt. Jess breathed deeply. She had to get used to saying it, so she might as well start practicing now. 'It's just...I recently broke up with someone, or he broke up with me, actually. I was supposed to be getting a ring on my finger this weekend...in Paris...but...' She shrugged. 'He fell in love with someone else.'

Elodie winced and touched Jess's arm. 'Wow, that sucks. I'm sorry to hear that.' They sat in silence for a moment and then she probed, 'But that doesn't explain the spontaneous thing.'

'Oh, that's because I—' She was about to say she was afraid that he broke up with her because he found her too unadventurous, but she decided to say, 'I'm trying to say yes instead of no all the time. Open myself up to new experiences.'

'Experiences like my brother.' Elodie smirked. Seriously, she reminded Jess of a dirty Audrey Hepburn.

'Like…your brother, yes.'

Elodie nudged her with her elbow. 'And was it everything you dreamed of and more?'

'Um. Uh. It was great. He's very…attentive.' God, did she want to stop having this conversation.

'Well, if you want to have any more spontaneous sexual experiences, let me know. My girlfriend has been begging me to do a threesome.'

If Jess had been drinking water, she would have spit it out. 'Oh, um. No…thank you? I mean, I'm flattered that you asked, but I don't think I'm feeling *that* spontaneous.'

She shrugged. 'Shame.'

Jess was dying to ask some questions of her own, like what he was doing that day and why he'd reacted as he did when Elodie forgot. However, that seemed a bit too personal and Jess didn't want to seem like she was snooping. However, there was another thing that had been bugging her for a while…

'How old is Gabriel?'

'Ha, this is going to blow your mind. He's 36. Yeah, I know. He acts 50.'

Doing the math, Jess realised he had been around her age when he lost his foot. Her heart ached for him. She couldn't stop thinking about how alone he must have felt.

On a similar train of thought, Elodie said, 'But I guess when you've been through what he's been through, it ages a person.'

72

'Did it...did it change him?' She didn't want to pry, but also she really wanted to know.

'Definitely.' She was uncharacteristically quiet for a moment. 'He went away a boy. Always so interested in other people, social...and came back...well...something else. A shadow of who he'd once been. I remember, before, he was the guy that everyone wanted to talk to at parties. The stories he told...I could see that he loved his job, even though I always hated it.'

Jess had trouble picturing the frowning man she'd met at the gallery in this role, the *raconteur*. He seemed so serious now.

Elodie continued, 'And then when he returned to us, he lost his spark. On top of that, the poor guy had to live with my parents while he waited for his prosthesis and learned how to be independent again. I mean, that would depress anybody. Our mom mourned the loss of his limb more than he did.'

'Do your parents live nearby?'

'They used to, but now they've retired to Martinique. They were in the process of moving when Gabriel had his accident. They stayed until he was back on his feet, literally, and then left. Personally, I think they couldn't handle seeing their son less than he'd been.' She huffed bitterly. 'The thing is, I don't even think it was losing his foot that broke him. It was what happened to Fatima, in my opinion. Although he's never told me the full story.'

Jess pursed her lips. Fatima...that must be the woman in the photograph. Jess wanted so badly to ask more questions, but felt that whatever happened to this woman was Gabriel's story to tell, not his sister's. Instead she said, 'So now it's up to you to take care of him.'

'I do my best. He doesn't make it easy.' Elodie glanced heavenwards. 'He's a lot better than he was. Finding his love of aerial photography helped. He took me up once, and I saw a glimpse of the brother I once knew up there. Carefree. Excited by life.' Jess agreed.

He had been a different person in the sky. 'But other than that, I never met a man so good at filling up his schedule with meaningless tasks. Like he's just biding time until he dies. When he's not travelling to take pictures, he's either reading or working or doing his stupid Japanese pottery thing or watering his plants or sitting upstairs in his man-cave listening to classical music on vinyl. Did he show it to you?'

'Um...no.' They had been busy exploring other things.

'It's like he's replaced human relationships with busywork.' She sighed. 'I invited him to my thirtieth birthday party a few months ago, and did he come? Of course not. Every time I asked him, he'd say *yes, yes, yes* and then on the night...nothing. My girlfriend is a psychiatrist and says that he should be in therapy. He was, for a long time. But he stopped a couple years ago. Seems to think he's cured, if that's even possible.'

Her gaze caught on a sign outside the bus. 'This is our stop!' Taking Jess's hand, she pulled her up, and they exited. 'The school is just up here,' she said, approaching a tree-lined road.

Jess was still processing everything that Elodie had told her about Gabriel. It was a lot to take in. For one thing, it confirmed to her that she shouldn't expect anything from him—also known as the number one rule in the one-night-stand handbook. But Elodie's revelations gave Jess a strange sense of...pride? Pride that she, a primary school teacher from London, had sparked some life in him and driven this reserved man wild in bed.

She had done that. The sense of power was new and a tiny bit intoxicating.

They entered the school grounds through a parking lot and made their way towards an immaculate green playing field. Whoever the groundskeeper was must have trained on a golf course. The school had carved out space for itself on a long stretch of land sandwiched between a motorway and an avenue. But the hum of cars was drowned out by a DJ playing a selection of that summer's pop anthems.

Along the edge of the playing field curved a succession of functional and modern school buildings. Compared to the independent school where she worked, this one had been built this century and had masses more space. Her school enjoyed great facilities, but not a lot of room. The kids had to walk ten minutes to get to their fields. Here, it was much more self-contained.

Colourful picnic blankets sat like patchwork on the field and some of the adults were manning a station of barbecues. The younger children who hadn't seen each other all summer ran around like pack animals whereas the older kids sat in circles far away from their parents.

A rotund, middle-aged woman with dark hair and glasses approached. Elodie introduced her as the Head of School and added, 'This is my brother's friend, Jess. She's an elementary teacher in England.'

'Ah,' said the woman with genuine interest. 'Where do you teach?'

Jess told her and the woman made an impressed face. 'Is John Shepherd still the head there?'

'Actually, yes. Wow! Do you know him?'

The woman's mouth twisted in a half-smile. 'Just tell him that Anna Wilkins said hi.' She winked and Jess wondered if there was a story there. The independent school world was small and everybody seemed to know each other, especially at the head level. Suddenly she had a vision of all the heads of all the schools meeting at a conference that was more like summer camp, with all the usual summer camp shenanigans. She giggled.

Elodie grabbed her hand and pulled her away.

'She seems nice,' said Jess.

'Oh, she's great. I really love working here.'

The next few hours passed in a fever of small talk with various parents who loved her accent, and sitting on the grass with Elodie while she told Jess funny teaching stories. Towards the end, Elodie took Jess into the school to show her the classroom where Elodie worked. It looked like...a classroom. A well-stocked one, but a classroom all the same, with pithy motivational sayings on the wall that said things like, 'The future of the world is in this room today.'

'I know, I know,' said Elodie when she caught Jess looking at it. 'But Americans love that kind of rah-rah shit.'

Jess smiled. 'No, it's great. I think we could use a bit more of that in our school.'

While Elodie went to use the toilet, Jess waited in the hallway, staring out of the windows facing the playing field. Some families were packing up their blankets, getting ready to do whatever people in Paris did on a Sunday afternoon. Jess planned to head to the Eiffel Tower and just walk around. She had read somewhere that walking was the thoroughest way to see a city. She wished she'd brought her running clothes with her; she would have been able to see twice as much in the same time. But she had packed for a proposal, not a marathon.

A rustling sound behind a nearby pillar drew her attention. Poking her head around it, she saw a boy—maybe seven years old— reading a picture book.

'Oh, hello there,' said Jess.

The boy startled, closed the book, and held it to his chest. He pressed himself back into the wall. Jess crouched down to his level, but made sure to maintain distance from him, not to crowd his space.

'It's all right. I'm Jess,' she said. The child just looked at her, brown eyes wide and blinking.

'That's a great book you're reading.' Shel Silverstein poems. As an author he wasn't as well known in the UK, but she had come across one of his stories in the library and loved the way he played with language. She read *The Giving Tree* to her class every year.

Lowering her voice, she recited a poem of Silverstein's about two people stuck together who couldn't stand each other or agree on anything. However, the moral was to look on the bright side because they might have been a threesome instead of a twosome. She finished, and a tentative smile played at the child's lips. He covered his mouth with his hand and laughed without making any noise.

'Well, that was something to behold,' Elodie said, joining Jess. She stood up. Looking down at the child, Elodie said, 'Hello, Ichiro, I think your parents are looking for you. Shall we go and find them?' She held out her hand and the child reluctantly got to his feet. Ignoring Elodie's hand, he slipped his into Jess's instead.

'Oh!' she said surprised and delighted at the same time. She loved making connections with children.

They descended the stairs together and returned to the field where Ichiro was reunited with his mother. Elodie said her goodbyes to her colleagues and the parents, and they walked back towards the tree-lined avenue.

'You're good,' said Elodie, cutting a glance towards Jess. 'You have a beautiful manner with children.' She pointed behind her. 'Ichiro has selective mutism. Apparently, he talks fine at home, but never at school.'

'I had a child like that in my class last year,' Jess said. 'She spoke Polish at home with no problems and she could understand English, but just didn't like speaking it in school. One day she said hello to me and I wanted to scream it from the rooftops.'

'Yeah, nothing feels as good as making a difference to someone.'

Jess's thoughts turned to Gabriel. His invitation to join him on the flight definitely made a difference to her. She wished she knew how to return the favour.

'Anyway,' said Elodie, 'I'm meeting my girlfriend and some

friends for an afternoon of too much wine and good food. You're more than welcome to join us?'

'Thank you, but I'm going to do some touristy things.' Tempting as the offer was, Jess needed some time alone to process everything that had happened in the past 72 hours. *The best therapy is a long walk*, her father always said. Also, she had monopolised enough of Elodie's time. As much as she enjoyed her company, Jess had the same feeling that had niggled at her earlier at Gabriel's, that feeling of being an interloper in somebody else's life. Jess had to remember how to live her own for a while.

Elodie gave Jess instructions on how to get to the Eiffel Tower and waited with her until her bus came along. With an affectionate hug and a kiss on each cheek, Elodie said, 'Well, if I don't see you again, have a lovely life, Jess. And thank you again for taking pity on my brother. If anyone needs a good lay, it's him.' She winked and Jess was glad to disappear into the bus, so Elodie couldn't see her sad frown.

Regret had already started to make a home in Jess's heart. Not regret that she'd slept with Gabriel—nothing could make her feel remorseful about that after how much she enjoyed it. No, the only thing she regretted was that they might not get to do it again.

9

THE DREAM ALWAYS STARTED THE SAME WAY.

Gabriel was lying on the dusty floor, blindfolded, his hands secured so tightly behind him with plastic zip ties that his circulation was practically cut off. His veins burned. He flexed his fingers trying to regain some feeling. It was no use asking the guards to loosen the ties. From experience, he'd found that requesting help only inspired further cruelties.

Outside the window, he heard the sound of children playing, the thump of a ball as it hit a foot, or a wall, or the ground. The young voices gave him hope, reminding him of a world that existed beyond this claustrophobic, airless room.

One of the villagers had thrown a rock at him yesterday, cutting him across his eyebrow. Now the blindfold stuck to his skin where the blood had crusted. He avoided thinking about the bacteria probably infecting his wound.

It was afternoon. Their captors had already led them on their daily parade, their hands at the end of rough ropes tied to the tail of a cantankerous donkey. If they didn't keep up with the donkey, the rope pulled its tail and it'd buck at them. Fatima had barely avoided having her knee kicked out.

Every day, the soldier moved the three prisoners through the village to a different hole in the wall. Or maybe it was the same one. Gabriel didn't know, nor did he care. He just hoped that among the villagers there might be somebody who sympathised, who might either tell somebody higher up, or in the best-case scenario, get word to the American army, that there were three journalists in captivity in the Hindu Kush.

It was his fault they were captured. It was him who thought the story they were chasing—of a big explosion somewhere in a Taliban-controlled area—was worth pursuing. And then as they got closer and some well-intentioned locals shared conflicting rumours about where they should go, they continued on, even though Gabriel's usually infallible gut warned him that perhaps it was time to turn around. He said as much.

'Are you losing your nerve?' joked Fatima. He should have insisted.

Their driver, a young man in his twenties, accidentally drove them straight into an ambush. He'd paid for it with his life. Nothing the Taliban hated more than other Afghanis helping out the heathen journalists, especially since the Taliban liked to control their own PR.

Outside the wooden door, Gabriel heard two voices. He called them Cheech and Chong because they were always stuffing *naswar*, a local type of addictive powdered tobacco, into their lower lips. The acrid smell was even stronger than their body odour. If Gabriel had anything of note in his stomach, he'd vomit it up.

But the dribble of water and the hard bread they were fed each day hardly touched the sides.

'You guys all right?' said Gabriel, his voice scratchy.

'Yes,' said Fatima.

'Top form,' said Johnson Lee, a photojournalist from London that Gabriel had known for years. Just last week, he had watched Johnson challenge and beat an arrogant US soldier in a push-up contest. Amazing how easily even Johnson had been subdued by their captors, his muscled arms useless in their plastic-tie handcuffs.

One of their captors shouted something in Pashto and the door creaked open. Gabriel's body trembled, a new Pavlovian response he'd developed to the sound of that door. It seldom meant anything good was going to happen.

He held his breath. Which one of them would they beat today? He didn't want them to choose Fatima. She'd already had more than her share of physical abuse from these men. Nothing sexual, thankfully. But when they'd taken the blindfolds off of the three of them earlier for the donkey parade, Gabriel had seen the bruises on her usually beautiful face. One of her cheekbones had caved in. She would need a plastic surgeon when they got out of here to rebuild it.

If they got out of here.

Wanting to draw the soldier's attention away from her, Gabriel tried to sit up. He would rather they beat him than her. Within seconds, he was rewarded with a swift kick in the ribs.

'You filthy dog,' said Cheech in heavily accented English. A ball of the man's pungent spit landed on Gabriel's forehead.

Good, he thought. *Come for me, you asshole.*

And then Fatima screamed.

Usually, that's where Gabriel would wake up, but tonight, maybe because it was her birthday, the nightmare's coils tightened around him.

JESS CRASHED ONTO HER BED, her feet tired after an afternoon and evening tramping the streets of Paris. The city was a walkable treasure trove; every corner she turned revealed a jewel to behold. Centuries blended into each other, like layers of silt. Marie Antoinette tumbled into Chopin who tumbled into Voltaire who tumbled into Coco Chanel. It was a historical box of *bonbons*.

The only slight downside to the afternoon was when she'd received a text from her father:

Anything you'd like to tell me?

This was followed by an explosion of excited emojis. She realised that he must have known about the proposal. Of course, Krish would have done things by the book and asked for her hand in marriage. Swallowing her pride, she pressed her dad's number on her phone and sat on a bench beneath the Eiffel Tower. The phone barely had time to ring when he answered.

'Hello, pumpkin! So should your mother buy a hat?' he asked. Jess could hear the excitement in his voice, which made her heart sink. Knowing him, he was already working on his speech.

'Um…not quite.' She breathed in and quickly spit out, 'Actually, we broke up.' Saying the words to her dad was hard, and tears flooded her eyes. The concept of Krish being her *ex*-boyfriend still seemed strange to her. Telling her dad made it real.

'What do you mean *broke up*? I thought—'

'I know, daddy. I don't really want to talk about it now, but he fell in love with somebody else. An ex-girlfriend.' She wiped her tears away. She didn't want to cry about this anymore.

'An ex…? What? But he…*Krish* did this?'

'Yup.' Her parents had loved Krish. She realised they'd be experiencing their own grief from losing him.

'Oh, well. That's…um…are you okay?'

'I'll be fine.' She rolled her eyes upwards and flapped her free hand to dry them.

'Why don't you come home this week? Let us take care of you.'

She winced. 'Actually, I'm in Paris.'

'What? By yourself? In a *foreign country*?' He said foreign country like she'd announced she was moving into a Bolivian prison. Her parents didn't travel much outside the UK. 'What are you doing *there*?'

A vision of Gabriel's head between her thighs passed through her mind and she blushed. 'Just…experiencing the culture.'

'Is it safe? I've heard there's a lot of knife crime.'

Jess snapped her tongue. 'No more than London, dad.'

'Okay, well…when are you back?'

'Thursday afternoon.' She imagined him marking his trusty calendar. Her father was one of the few people who still kept a paper diary instead of a digital one.

He sighed. 'Okay, text me every day to let me know you're safe and…see you next weekend?'

'Yes, dad. Love to you and mum.' She kissed the air and then hung up. A small smile played at her lips. No matter how old she got, she would always feel like their little girl, and she was grateful for their unconditional love.

Her shoulders relaxed. She hadn't realised how stressed she was about telling her parents, but now that it was done, she could move on.

At least she hadn't starting sobbing while talking to him. Great progress already.

After that, she'd walked away from the the Eiffel Tower, towards the Louvre. Maybe tomorrow, she'd buy a ticket to see the Mona Lisa.

Next, she'd wandered to the Arc de Triomphe and, finally, past the Moulin Rouge. Pigalle, the area surrounding the red windmill, surprised her—not because of the abundant sex shops and erotic museums; she expected those. It was the tired feeling of Pigalle, like the whole district stayed too long at the party. Even the infamous Moulin Rouge in all its gaudy glory made her feel sad for a bygone age in ways that other parts of Paris hadn't.

Climbing the stairs towards the Sacre Coeur, she was delighted to find a fire juggler entertaining tourists on the basilica steps, with all of Paris and her lights stretching out in the distance behind him. Jess watched him twirl his fire wands for a while and dropped some euros into his hat before continuing on. Around the corner from her flat, a clothing shop tempted her inside with its boho window display, and she bought two casual dresses, a pair of embroidered jean shorts, and a couple of peasant blouses.

All in all, she'd clocked over 35,000 steps on her watch.

Back on the bed in her flat, her stomach gurgled happily in memory of the three-course dinner she'd eaten. She'd restricted herself to one glass of excellent French wine and read a book as she dined alone. She enjoyed the experience more than she thought she would. There was something satisfying about doing exactly what she wanted, when she wanted—no one else's needs to consider. She wasn't used to it, but maybe she should do more of it. *Self care*, Krish's sister, Ankita, called it. She loved going to spas for self-care weekends and had invited Jess along a few times.

Thinking of Ankita threw a momentary pall over her happy glow. Jess had thought they'd be sister-in-laws in a year's time. How swiftly life changed. One second you're about to get engaged; the next, you're flying over Paris in a helicopter and letting a gorgeous Frenchman dine out on your body.

As much as mulling over the reasons for the demise of her relationship occupied her, the memory of last night also wouldn't leave her alone. She'd thought about it on and off all day long, still blushing when some of the ways she'd allowed him to pleasure her flickered behind her eyes. Who knew that a finger up the bum could be so...effective. She would never have let Krish or any of her other exes do that.

Paris has changed you, she thought and laughed.

Stripping out of her sundress and bra, she slid into a rosy pink camisole and matching shorts. Engagement pyjamas. She'd bought some seriously amazing undergarments for this trip. The sensation of the silk against her skin did nothing to calm the raging awareness of her own body that last night's memories had stirred up in her.

She brushed her teeth and crawled into bed, checking the time on her alarm clock. Eleven o'clock.

I wonder if Gabriel is awake.

The thought landed in her head like a well-aimed dart. She curled up under the covers and tried to get comfortable, but the words kept repeating in her head.

What if he was upstairs, wondering if she was downstairs? She didn't have his number, so couldn't call him. He said he'd call her if he had time, but...it was Sunday night. What if he was just being polite?

After everything that Elodie had told her about him, Jess wanted to see him again, to hold him in her arms. Maybe even to go all the way with him.

She giggled and covered her face with her hand. *All the way?!* What was she? A teenager?

Still, once she admitted it to herself, the idea wouldn't leave her alone. What harm would it cause? She was leaving in a few days. They would both get on with their lives, and she'd have new memories to warm herself on cold winter nights.

Besides, at present, she was Yes Jess!

Throwing the covers off, she placed her feet on the floor with conviction: she was going to knock on his door. Jess grabbed a cardigan and wrapped it around herself, not because she was cold, but just in case she ran into anyone in the hallway. Her camisole wasn't exactly opaque.

On tiptoes, she crept out of her flat and pulled the door closed behind her. Her feet padded across the cold checkered tiles towards the lift. *What am I doing?* This felt delightfully naughty for someone who had followed the rules her whole life.

A huge smile cut across her face. The lift doors opened and she was mortified to see a couple in their seventies already in there, dressed like they'd just come back from a show. Closing her eyes and pursing her lips, Jess stepped into the lift and spent an awkward minute staring at the ascending numbers on the panel next to the door. These people hadn't been born yesterday, and she practically had Booty Call written on her forehead.

The lift stopped at the sixth floor and the couple got out. As she left, the woman winked at Jess and gave her a knowing nod. Jess wanted to die. Could this be any more humiliating?

She got out on the top floor and stood in front of Gabriel's door, chewing on her lip and staring at the handle. Now that she was here, doubt slithered through her. A number of scenarios presented themselves like a slide show in her head.

1. He's not home.
2. He's home, but he's not interested.
3. He's home, but there's somebody already with him.

Sugar honey iced tea. She hadn't even considered that last one until now. What if there was another woman in there? It was possible.

But in her heart, she knew there wasn't. She remembered that morning, when she'd implied that she was nobody to him, and he'd turned to her and said: *'That's not true. You're somebody.'* Those words had shot straight to her heart.

Jess took a deep breath and blew it out fast. It was now or never. With renewed sense of purpose, she knocked on his door and waited for a minute. No answer. Perhaps she hadn't knocked hard enough. She did it again.

Still no answer.

She pressed her ear to the wood, listening for any sound. She couldn't hear anything.

Her shoulders slumped with disappointment. It had taken a lot to work herself up to come to his flat. She had once heard an interview on Radio 4 where Susie Dent coined the phrase *'anticipointment.'* That's what Jess felt now: the perfect marriage of anticipation and disappointment.

With a frown, she turned to go.

That's when she heard the scream.

10

WITHOUT THINKING, JESS DIALLED THE CODE FOR GABRIEL'S DOOR, which she had thanks to her obsessive need for clean teeth.

Once inside, she heard the strangled scream again. 'Fatima!'

She had no doubt it was Gabriel, and he was in pain. She had never heard anything like it before: primal and bleak. As she rushed past the kitchen island, she clocked the bottle of whiskey and the single empty glass sitting next to it.

In his bedroom, she found him thrashing in his sheets, his hands clenched in the duvet, his brow furrowed, and his eyes squeezed shut. The bathroom light was on, casting a tungsten glow across the bottom of his bed. His prosthesis lay abandoned on the floor, as though he'd taken it off and tossed it down in disgust.

Jess bounced from foot to foot, unsure what to do. She'd read somewhere that she shouldn't try to wake him. Or was that sleep walking? She shook her hands in uncertainty. Maybe if she just held him and talked to him calmly, that might help. He seemed tense, but not violent.

'No! Not her,' he shouted.

Curling her fingers into fists and coming to a decision, she lifted the duvet and slid into the bed next to him. She arranged the pillow so her head would be slightly above his. Delicately, she manoeuvred her body next to his, her hand gliding across his bare, sweaty chest. She wiggled her other arm under his head, and he whimpered in his sleep. She smelled the sharp tang of whiskey and fear on him.

'Shhh,' she whispered close to his ear. 'It's okay. You're okay.'

Gabriel cried out again, an expression of utter agony on his face.

Jess pulled him to her and stroked his head, repeating the same words over and over again.

His body shook. She absorbed it.

She kept reassuring him and holding him gently, sailing on pure instinct. She'd never been in this situation before. Sure, she had soothed friends over broken hearts, lost competitions, jobs they didn't get...but this was something else entirely. It was brutal. And real. And all-encompassing. A mental prison. All she had to help him was her body and her words, so that's what she used.

Time ticked by and she had no idea how long passed before he began to settle. It felt like hours, but was probably closer to thirty minutes. Finally, his breathing evened out, and he stopped squirming, his chest rising and falling in a normal rhythm.

Jess watched over him. After what Elodie had told her, Jess could only imagine what happened to him in Afghanistan, what sort of nightmare he relived in his sleep. *Fatima*, he had called out. Elodie had mentioned her, too. Jess's eyes immediately turned to the picture on the mantelpiece. Had Gabriel been in love with her? How did she die? Did he have to watch it happen?

She squeezed her eyes closed, trying not to let her imagination run away with the possibilities. It put her break-up with Krish into acute perspective. Sure, it had been upsetting and she missed him. But nobody had died. They'd both survive and go on living their lives.

Oh, Gabriel. What happened to you? She kissed his temple.

Hugging him to her, Jess continued her vigil over him, forcing herself to stay awake even when her own eyelids wanted to close.

GABRIEL AWOKE WITH A START.

Where was he and why did he smell strawberries?

He'd had the dream again. Guilt washed through him, as it always did when he realised that Fatima would never feel safe again and that he had failed to protect her.

It had been a while since he'd suffered through that particular nightmare in such excruciating detail—from the intense, wet hay stench of the *naswar* to the tickle of the bugs' tiny feet crawling over his legs to the searing pain when the bullet obliterated his right foot.

But there had been something different about this dream, too. An unexpected presence.

He looked down. The first thing he saw was the manicured hand resting on his chest, the fingers tangled in the crinkly black and grey hairs. A smooth leg intertwined with his own. The sound of someone else's soft breathing tickled his ear. Turning his head, he was surprised to see Jess, her beautiful face relaxed, her lips gently parted, her curly mane spread across the pillow behind her.

Now he remembered. She had been in his dream, too, towards the end. When he was screaming after Fatima died and the young Taliban soldier shot him, unexpectedly Jess had appeared. Afghanistan had faded to black. In the dark void, she took him in her arms and told him everything would be all right. Her calming words sank into him, rescuing him from the precipice. Now, he understood she had been there in real life.

Jess came for him.

A feeling he hadn't allowed himself to have in a long time burned in his heart.

Jᴇss's ᴇʏᴇʟɪᴅs ғʟᴜᴛᴛᴇʀᴇᴅ ᴏᴘᴇɴ.

Gabriel faced her, his head propped up on his hand, his brown eyes trained on her face. '*Bonjour,*' he said, his face unreadable.

'Um, morning,' she said, and stretched, using it as an excuse to move away from him and give him some space. She had, after all, broken into his house and crawled into bed with him last night.

As though wanting to stop her from leaving, he reached out his large, warm hand and placed it on her waist, under her silky camisole. He rubbed his thumb back and forth. Goose pimples erupted all over her skin, just like they had the first time he touched her there. 'Did you know that, in France, we still use the guillotine for trespassers?'

'Is that so?' She felt a blush creep up her neck.

'Good thing I'm not planning to press charges.'

'I'm sorry...it's just that I came upstairs because, well...'—*because I wanted to screw your brains out*—'because I wanted to see if you were home, and I heard you screaming...'

'It's fine. It happens sometimes.'

Her brow creased in a frown. 'Gabriel, what I saw last night was not *fine.*' Would he want to talk about it? She wouldn't push him because it was none of her business, even though she cared. She'd take her lead from him.

He flinched and his hands tightened on her waist. For a moment, she wondered if sex would help him feel better. It wasn't necessarily the circumstances in which she wanted to sleep with him, but she would do it, if it helped Gabriel. That's what she'd wanted from him last night, anyway, when she came to his flat. Did it matter if the *why* had changed?

They stared at each other, with no sound except for their breathing. In his eyes, she identified desire warring with other emotions in the way his eyelids flickered and refocused on her. Jess wondered how she'd ever thought this man was cold. He was just damaged and trying to protect himself. She wanted to protect him, too.

Gabriel swayed towards her—just a centimetre—and her lips parted. But then he seemed to have second thoughts, sighed, and rolled onto his back. He squeezed his eyes shut and massaged his temple with his ring finger and thumb.

'I need to get out of Paris for a few days,' he said to the ceiling. 'Sometimes, this place feels too claustrophobic.'

'Oh. Of course.' Disappointment reared within her and her heart dropped. She was leaving on Thursday. If he went away until Wednesday, then that would pretty much be the end of her trip. But she knew the deal: this had been a no-strings-attached transaction. He didn't owe her anything.

That didn't stop it from hurting. *You idiot, Jess!* How had she gotten so invested, so fast? And yet, here she was, caring about this man, and the fact that he didn't feel the same way about her unexpectedly distressed her. 'I understand.'

She started to sit up when his hand wrapped around her wrist.

'Wanna come with me?'

As GABRIEL'S black SUV sped down the motorway through the patchwork countryside southwest of Paris, Jess imagined she was in a getaway car, whisking her away to a secret location for an illicit rendezvous. All she needed was a pair of oversized sunglasses and a scarf to wrap around her hair à la Grace Kelly.

It was almost perfect, like a scene from a movie. The only issue...? Classical music played on the radio and Jess made a yuck face. It wasn't really her thing. 'Do you mind if I change this?'

Gabriel placed his hand over his heart as though mortally wounded. 'You mean, you don't like Beethoven?'

'No.'

'Mozart?'

'Nope.'

'Debussy?'

She laughed. 'You can name all the dead composers in the world, but I'm going to keep saying no. Sorry.'

He huffed. 'Fine, change it. But this conversation isn't over.' She twirled the dial until she found a pop station playing Taylor Swift—ironically, it was 'Getaway Car', a song about a rebound relationship. This time, Gabriel made a yuck face, and she laughed. She couldn't imagine a singer that would be less on his radar (but who totally should be).

Jess still couldn't believe she was doing this, heading out of town with a man she barely knew and yet knew so well in other ways. He still hadn't said anything about last night. She figured he would talk to her when he was ready...if he was ever ready. Maybe he never would be. It wasn't like she was his girlfriend or anything. Her chest tightened with a feeling she was loathe to name.

As if compelled, her head tipped towards him. She studied his straight nose and full lips, which she could feel on her body if she closed her eyes. He looked so handsome in his linen top and aviator sunglasses, with his hair newly washed, his stubble recently shaved, and his woodsy cologne freshly applied. He wore shorts, his prosthetic leg fully visible to her. His clothes choice gave her the impression he felt comfortable in her presence—a thought that made her inordinately happy.

The further they got from Paris, the more relaxed he became: his shoulders began to unknot and his jaw unclenched. He even laughed at a joke she told about pirates; she'd heard about a million of them from her kids: *A slice of pie costs $2.00 in Jamaica and $3.50 in the Bahamas. These are the pie rates of the Caribbean.*

She grinned.

Gabriel caught her eyes on him and gifted her with a rare curve of his lips. 'What?'

'Nothing. I just like looking at you.' Her stomach fluttered as she said it. The words bordered on intimate, but who were they kidding? They were undeniably attracted to each other. They'd be having sex at some point in the next couple of days—hopefully, sooner rather than later. Couldn't get much more intimate than that.

His smile turned wolfish and a ball of heat exploded between her legs. He reached over and took her hand in his, bringing it to his lips for the briefest of kisses.

I could get used to this, she thought and immediately slapped the sentiment away. This was a fling. Rebound sex. Nothing more.

'So where are we going?' she asked to take her mind in a different direction.

'I have a small place in the country,' he explained as he turned off the motorway. 'It's a fixer upper, but I needed a project, so it keeps me busy.'

Jess remembered what Elodie had said about all the ways he kept himself occupied to avoid human interaction. This sounded like another one to add to the list.

They passed through a village populated by stone houses with colourful shutters and green creepers covering the facades. She imagined that, if she Googled 'quaint French village', pictures of this place would pop up. There was even a man with a beret and a baguette walking a poodle. *Seriously?!*

A few miles down the road, Gabriel pulled into a rocky drive that wove through a forest. The tires crunched on gravel. A pair of doves launched themselves into the tree canopy as the car approached them, and a squirrel raced across their path. Emerging from the woods, they passed through an iron gate with an ivy-covered stone wall on either side.

In front of her loomed a magnificent grey house. She counted three floors behind a round turret with a conical hat at the top. A petite Cinderella staircase hugged the turret on both sides, each leading up to an entrance.

Her jaw dropped open. 'I thought you said it was small. This is a *chateau.*'

'Welcome to Château de la Plénitude,' he said, enjoying her surprise. 'My home away from home.'

'It's beautiful.'

He parked the car in front of a crumbling wall and some rusty barrels, and she scrambled out, eager to get inside, while he retrieved their bags from the boot.

Jess loved old things. At home she had a collection of antique teddy bears and vintage cookie jars. She adored watching shows about people refurbishing centuries-old buildings. While Krish preferred a Friday night film, she would sit next to him on the sofa with her headphones in, devouring restoration videos on YouTube. This chateau filled her with giddy delight.

Gabriel slung his backpack over one shoulder and picked up Jess's suitcase. He led her up the left set of stairs and she marvelled out loud about the immaculate stonework.

'It took ages. First, I had to scrub each stone with acid and then power wash them to clean them and get the old mortar out. Then I had to remix new mortar and colour match it and even out the steps.' His face lit up as he talked about his project.

Jess pictured it: Gabriel, shirtless, his powerful, sweaty chest glistening in the Loire sunshine, his strong, capable hands lifting the stones and reshaping the stairs.

'Sounds like a big job,' she said a little more breathlessly than intended.

'Everything in this chateau is a big job. Even the ones you think are going to be little jobs.'

She wondered if his leg ever got in the way, if it took him longer because of it. 'What's its history?'

He pulled out an oversized skeleton key from his bag and Jess almost squealed at the sheer perfection of it. 'It was built in the 18th century. Before I bought it, it had been abandoned for almost 50 years.' He turned the key in the lock. 'Ready to see inside? I'm warning you—there's still a lot to do. And this is a working holiday. You're going to have to muck in.'

'Sounds idyllic,' she said honestly.

The door creaked open and he stood aside so she could enter first, straight into a wood-panelled hallway. A painted portrait of a sour-faced French aristocrat hung on the wall. His frown reminded her of someone.

'Relative of yours?' she joked.

'Very funny. I found it at a flea market. Thought it worked with the decor.'

Next, her eyes followed the spiral staircase twirling up inside the turret. 'Wow.'

'Tour or food first?'

She checked her watch. It was close to dinner time, but she really wanted to see the place. 'Definitely the tour.'

Gabriel laughed. 'What the lady wants. Let me just take the bags upstairs and I'll join you in a minute.' She wondered if she should offer to do it for him because of his leg, but he was already halfway up the first flight and seemed to be managing just fine.

Jess walked through the doorway across the hall and found herself standing in a huge, high-ceilinged reception room. Peeling patterned wallpaper wilted like dying flowers, exposing crumbling plaster. The time-worn floor needed re-sanding and varnishing, and a once-glorious chandelier resting in the corner could use a good polishing. But Jess saw its potential.

When he caught up to her, she was spinning around in the middle of the room, imagining what it could be one day: a couple of Persian rugs to create different spaces. A set of slouchy sofas set around an antique coffee table. Chairs in a more formal French style to contrast. She pictured it so clearly. She had to remind herself that this wasn't her project, and she'd only be here for a few days. Gabriel wasn't her boyfriend. She lived in London.

Still, it was fun to pretend. 'What will you do with this room? Perfect place for a ball.'

'Obviously. I love dancing.' His voice dripped with sarcasm.

She tilted her head to the side and held out her hand to him. 'Maybe you just need the right partner.' After she said it she blushed, realising it sounded like she meant *the right girlfriend.* 'For dancing, I mean,' she clarified.

He hesitated before stepping towards her and sliding his left palm against hers. In a surprise move, he spun her around and then clasped her to him, swaying her back and forth.

Jess laughed. 'I can see monsieur already has some moves.' Their eyes connecting, Jess leaned towards him and tilted her head for a kiss.

He didn't disappoint. His hands cupped her face, and his lips moved over hers. Heat flared between them, her breasts turning heavy with desire to be touched. The desperation in their kiss increased, and she pressed herself closer to him, but then he suddenly stopped and stepped away, leaving her gasping for breath. He rubbed his jaw and his brow knitted. She had trouble reading him. 'Um…I'll show you the library next.' He turned on his heel and exited the room.

And then…? she thought, biting her lip and following him,

wondering why he'd put the brakes on. Maybe he really wanted to show off the chateau first? Now that she had decided to have sex with him, she wanted it yesterday, especially because she'd already had the taster session a couple of nights ago. Everything about him was causing her pheromones to go into overdrive. If they were visible, they'd be surrounding her like a cloud. Seriously, she wouldn't be surprised if men from the neighbouring village started turning up like amorous zombies, unsure what had led them there, but horny as hell.

But...tour first.

GET A GRIP, *Gabriel.*

He marched towards the library, determined to put some space between Jess and him.

Never had he wanted a woman so badly, yet been so conflicted about acting on it. Strange emotions swirled within him. Emotions he didn't want. Emotions that scared him.

He liked her laugh just a little too much. The curve of her lips. The way her whole face lit up when she smiled. How his heart beat faster when she touched him.

Then, while he was kissing her, he'd had a vision: Jess was standing in that very room when it was finished, wearing a yellow sundress, her hair loose, her skin tanned and healthy, a smile on her face...and a baby on her hip. His baby. She looked so happy and natural in that setting, like it had been made just for her.

The thought physically pained him. Because for the first time, he wanted that, but he could never have it.

Gabriel reminded himself that none of this was real. Jess wasn't looking for anything serious. She'd just had her heart broken, for chrissakes. He was Rebound Guy.

And as for him, he couldn't risk anyone relying on him. Not a wife and most certainly not a child.

He'd only let them down.

Cry me a river, said Fatima's voice in his head. *You're so fucking dramatic sometimes.*

Shut up, he told her.

What were they doing here? When he'd invited Jess, it had seemed like the perfect solution. For just a moment, he thought it would be a nice break to step out of his life, to spend a few days pretending to be lord of the manor with a beautiful woman in his bed.

But she was getting too close to him.

Now they were here, he couldn't shake this awkward feeling, like the joke was on him. Upstairs, he had put their bags into separate bedrooms, not wanting to commit to sleeping in the same bed as her, even though they'd already done that, twice. For some reason, the thought of doing it here felt like a dangerous line to cross. Playing happy families.

Bringing Jess to his chateau had been a mistake.

You deserve some happiness, you douche, said Fatima, using her favourite pet name for him.

That's where they disagreed.

11

AFTER THE KISS, JESS WAS DISAPPOINTED TO FIND THAT GABRIEL WAS all business as he explained the different stages of his renovations so far, from the complex structural work and electrics to his vision for the interior. He showed her the library, the only finished room on that floor. With its dark blue walls, shelves full of books and vinyl records, and the pricey sound system, it definitely had single-man aesthetic. 'I needed at least one place where I could relax when I came here,' he said. Jess eyed up the slouchy velvet couch against the wall and thought it looked relaxing all right…and a great place for a fumble and a cheeky blow job.

Unleashing the new bold, powerful version of herself, she grabbed his hand and tugged him towards the sofa, the gleam in her eye communicating her intentions.

He pulled away, stuffed his hands in his pockets, and said, 'You'll want to see the original bread oven. It's, um, in the kitchen.' And he spun around and walked briskly out of the room. She threw her arms in the air, eyebrows dipped with concern and confusion. What the hell was going on? Had she read this wrong? Did he bring her here to share his love of chateau restoration or to shag?

She followed him out of the room.

Indeed, it was an old brick bread oven. In a kitchen.

Even though she was interested in all of it, Jess felt like she was on a museum tour, and every time she manoeuvred herself next to Gabriel or attempted to take his hand, he'd move away from her like proximity wasn't professional. Or she had cooties, as her kids might say.

Had she done something wrong? Being in a steady relationship for two years, she'd forgotten the rollercoaster of doubt that often came with getting to know somebody new. Sure, it was fun finding out what made somebody tick, but the flip side was the constant analysis and uncertainty.

Not that this *was* a relationship. *It's just a fling*, she reminded herself.

As they finished exploring the second floor, ready to climb the stairs towards the finished bedrooms, Gabriel suggested, 'Why don't we abandon the tour for now and I'll make us some dinner?' Before she said yes or no, he was down the stairs and out the front door heading to the car for the bags of food he'd brought.

She thought they could spread out a blanket on the floor in the ballroom and have a picnic, light some candles to add some romance, but Gabriel had other plans. Instead, they sat at a wobbly plastic table in his makeshift kitchen and suffered through stilted conversation paired with bread, cheese, olives, salad, and wine.

After listening to him speak at length about insulation, she finally roused the courage to ask, 'Is everything all right?'

He froze, his eyes turning wary as he tore another chunk off the baguette. 'Yes...?'

'You just seem a little...' Brooding? Grumpy? Uninterested? '...distant.'

'I'm tired from the drive down. And everything.'

And then she felt bad because, of course, he'd had a rough night thanks to his nightmare. He was probably preoccupied with thoughts of Fatima, the woman he loved, not Jess. She'd been selfish, only thinking of her own desires instead of considering Gabriel's state of mind. *Do better,* she admonished herself.

After dinner, he told Jess to wait for him in the library while he cleaned up. Jess objected, wanting to help, but he insisted.

'I'll do it faster by myself,' he said and so, she left.

In the library, Jess sipped her wine and studied the books on his shelves, her fingers prancing over the spines: Henri Cartier Bresson, Phillip Jones Griffiths, Diane Arbus, Yann Arthus-Bertrand, Dorothea Lange...she stopped on a book of Magnum war photographs and pulled it off the shelf. She read the first paragraph of the forward, which talked about Magnum's creator, Robert Capa, who captured the best recorded evidence of the D-Day landings. She wondered if her great-grandfather might be one of the shaky figures in his photographs. From Capa's bio, she learned that, of the one hundred and six photos he took, only eight survived because an over-excited lab tech accidentally used too much heat on the negatives, melting them. Jess's breath caught as she read that; imagine experiencing what Capa went through and then losing the work. It made her feel sick.

On a hunch, she turned to the table of contents and perused the names. And there it was: Gabriel Severin. Her heart beat faster. Putting her glass down on the side table and turning on the lamp, she sat on the sofa and went straight to his pages.

She didn't know what to expect: pictures of people fighting, she assumed. His amazing aerial shots were the only evidence she had seen of his work. She already knew he had talent, but she didn't know how that would translate into his coverage of combat.

Page 102. Gabriel Severin.

'Severin's work is marked by the personal way he captured the stories of people in conflict. First and foremost, he was a human being, treating his subjects as fellow human beings instead of nameless specimens to be documented. He got close; he formed relationships; he gained trust. Whether documenting life on an American army base, rebels during the Arab Spring, or children affected by war in Sierra Leone, his portraits always tell a story, giving insight into the subject's state of mind. His photographs remind the viewer that we are all connected by the very fact of belonging to the same species. Severin retired from combat photography after losing his foot in Afghanistan.'

A picture of him accompanied the text, credited to Fatima Ahmad. He was sitting next to a young boy somewhere in the Middle East, playing a game of chess. The boy grinned and Gabriel laughed at the camera, as though the person taking the photo said something funny. He was younger, his hair fully black, his eyebrow unscarred. He was a man in his prime.

Before even turning the page, Jess had tears in her eyes.

The first portraits made her catch her breath: on the left, a US soldier, scared and tired, holding his helmet in his hand and cradling his head in his palm, his skin marked by dirt, and smoke billowing in the distance. Jess could hear the bombs, feel the fear. Opposite, another picture of US soldiers, relaxed, hanging out in camp, lifting weights and joking with each other. Next page. A young boy in Congo, wearing fatigues and carrying a rifle, his gaze hard but his stern countenance contradicted by a single tear falling down his cheek. Opposite: another young man in Sierra Leone, one eye missing but his face animated, caught in the act of telling a story.

Jess flipped through page after page of Gabriel's work. With each image, it made her see the man clearer and clearer. Gabriel was kind. Gabriel was brave. Gabriel was loving. Gabriel was…

…standing in the doorway, staring at her. 'What are you doing?'

She snapped the book closed, feeling like a naughty child caught rifling through the teacher's desk. 'Sorry. I saw it on the shelf and I…I just wanted to see…um…anyway, you didn't mention you were a Magnum photographer. That's pretty amazing.' She didn't know much, but she knew Magnum was a hard club to join.

His hands clenched and unclenched. Emotions flickered across his face: anger, pain, fear. She saw he was struggling. Pushing the book aside, she stood and went to him, gently taking his hand in hers. He let her. She pulled him over to the sofa and sat next to him. She made sure to position herself on his left because she had noticed over time that he preferred her on the opposite side to his prosthesis. Holding his hand in hers, she stroked it, massaging the fingers and palm to help him relax.

Eventually, he said, 'Sorry. I haven't looked at my old portfolio in a long time.'

'Your images…they're not what I was expecting.'

He shrugged. 'I just shot things as I saw them.'

'I can see that. Your portraits are so…so raw.'

Picking up the book, he gripped it so hard his knuckles turned white and he lowered it onto his lap. With a determined exhalation, he opened it straight to his page. His eyes lingered on his picture, his finger brushing Fatima's credit. He skimmed his write-up and grunted as he got to the end. 'Because of my foot,' he read. 'Their copywriter makes it sound like I just misplaced it. Anyway, I didn't quit because of my foot. I quit because I was done.'

'Because…because of Fatima.'

His body stiffened, and he nodded.

'Tell me about her,' said Jess, curling her feet under herself and smoothing some stray locks of hair off his temple.

He dropped the book onto the floor with a thud and leaned back on the sofa. Jess snuggled into him, rested her head on his shoulder, and waited for him to speak. In her experience with children, they found it easier to talk about difficult subjects during a walk, or sitting on a swing, or any situation where she and the child looked at something other than each other.

Jess continued to stroke his hand, keeping her gaze on his fingers. She didn't want to spook him.

After a minute, he said, 'Fatima was fearless. She had a nose for a story like nothing I've ever seen and a great eye. She was also wise and funny and irreverent. She was the best friend I ever had...and I couldn't save her.' His voice caught, and he continued to stare at the ceiling as he spoke. 'We met at a hotel bar in Kabul when we were both new to the job. We were in this room full of hardened photo-journalists, legends of the industry and we were just these new kids...still wet behind the ears. One of the other guys—he was known for being a sex pest—he put his hand on her ass and I stepped in to say something. But she had it covered. Before I even opened my mouth, she kneed him in the balls and lit a cigarette. After that I bought her a drink and that was it. We were a team.'

Jess pictured this beautiful, vivacious woman who ate risk for breakfast and saw opportunity in disaster. The kind of woman Jess wished she was more like. Was it possible to be jealous of a dead woman? Because that's the only way that Jess could describe the slippery feeling in her belly, and she felt guilty for it.

'We didn't always get to work on the same assignments, but we did whenever we could. Fatima and I always pushed each other to be better photographers. She encouraged me to go in my own direction with my style, not to follow the herd. As usual, she was always one hundred percent right.' His voice hitched, and he descended into silence. Jess didn't say a word.

He drew a shuddering breath. 'Except the one time she wasn't.'

Everything was hushed. Jess barely dared to breathe, afraid to interrupt him telling the story he needed to get out.

'We were in the mountains in the northeast of Afghanistan. There were three of us: me, Johnson Lee—a journo from London—and Fatima. She was on assignment with *Le Monde;* I was there for *The New York Times.* We had heard about a village that the Taliban had decimated, but no one had the story yet. Johnson insisted his intel was good and we were sharing a driver, so we all went or none of us went. I wanted to turn around. Usually, it was me pushing us to the brink of danger, but this time...my gut just said we should go back. But Fatima's told her we should keep going. She said, let's just drive forward another kilometre and see if we could find anyone with more info.' He banged his head backward on the cushion. 'I should have listened to my own intuition.'

'It was my second time being kidnapped. A downside of the job. As it was happening, I naively thought this time would be similar to the first. A few days of getting the shit beaten out of us, then negotiations, and release. But...' he paused, '...I knew pretty quickly that this was different.'

He quietened, his gaze shifting inward. Jess shuddered to think what atrocity he was watching, the movie in his mind. Elodie told Jess that Gabriel never spoke about what happened in Afghanistan. She could see why. It took a lot of courage to go back there.

After a minute of silence, Gabriel went on. 'These guys who took us, they were young...angry...untrained. Didn't care that we had value for a trade...they just hated us. Kept calling us dogs. Taunting us. They especially hated Fatima, because she was brown like them. Born Muslim, although she didn't practice.

'They kept us hostage for four days.' He shook his head and laughed with no humour. 'At least that's how long they told me it was...after. It's hard to know when you're wearing a blindfold. Every so often they'd move us to a different location in the village. They'd take off our blindfolds, tie us to the tail of a donkey in a row, always in the same order: Fatima, Johnson, me at the back. And then they'd parade us around. I kept thinking, surely, word would get back to somebody that this is going on.' Breathing deeply, he said, 'Some villagers threw rocks at us. That's how I got this.' He pointed to his eyebrow. Jess longed to kiss the scar, but supressed the urge. She didn't want to interrupt his flow.

'The places they kept us were always dry and dusty. Nothing to sleep on. No blankets. The days were warm—maybe 70 degrees—but the nights were freezing. At least they let us lie next to each other at night, for body heat. Somebody was always watching us or nearby. Usually in pairs. They would take it in turns to hit us. Fatima—' he choked on the word. 'They did their worst to her. I actually heard her arm snap. After they did it, one of them called his wife on his cell phone, to...to *brag...*'

Jess didn't need him to say any more. Tears were leaking from his eyes, hers as well, and she could just picture what they'd done to his girlfriend.

'I heard her pleading with them not to touch her. I tried to stop them, but my hands were tied behind my back. So tight, I could barely feel my fingers. I dislocated my shoulder trying to get myself free. They just laughed. And Fatima...she told me to stop. Didn't want me to get myself killed.' He ran his thumbs under both his eyes, as though by wiping the tears, he might also wipe away the memories.

'On the fourth day, I remember the children stopped playing. Outside our cell. Usually we could hear them through the window. It was the only pleasure we had. These young voices, laughing. The sound gave me hope. Anyway, on this day, they disappeared and I sensed that something was up. Then suddenly all hell broke loose. I heard American voices shouting, and then machine gun fire. Thinking we were alone in the hut, I managed to wiggle over to Fatima and bit off her blindfold with my teeth. She did the same for me. Her face...both her eyes were black and blue. She had bruises up and down her arms. Johnson's lips was split and his nose, completely busted. Seconds later, one of the kidnappers came in, eyes crazy, waving his gun around, shouting. Fatima tried to reason with him—she spoke fluent Pashto—but...' He paused for a moment. '...But he shot her. Right in the heart. I started screaming, so he shot me too. Blew my foot right off. Then somebody shot him. And I passed out.

'Next thing I knew, I was in a hospital in Kabul. A week had passed. My foot and half my lower leg was gone. Fatima was gone,' he whispered.

Jess said, 'I can't imagine what it's like to lose someone you love like that. It's horrible.' Now she completely understood his nightmares. 'But there was nothing you could have done to save her.'

Gabriel squeezed his eyes tight. 'I could have insisted we turn back.'

'You didn't know the future any more than she did.' Jess didn't want to say what she was thinking, that it was a dangerous job, and Fatima would have known the risks.

He lifted his head and looked down at Jess. 'Yesterday was her birthday. I spent the day with her wife and daughter, marking it, like we do every year. Johnson usually comes, too, but he's on assignment. He didn't quit, like I did.'

'Wife and daughter?' Jess said in surprise. 'I thought...I thought she was your lover.' She had assumed that best friend meant soulmates.

He huffed a laugh. 'Are you kidding me? That would have been like sleeping with my sister.'

Warring emotions rolled through her: relief that Fatima wasn't the love of his life, and self-reproach at even thinking that it mattered. It didn't affect the pain he felt. But was it wrong that Jess was glad that Gabriel wasn't pining for a lost love? It was hard to compete with a ghost. *Not that I'm competing*, she reminded herself.

She reached up and cupped his cheek in her hand. 'Thank you for telling me.' Her thumb stroked the shadowy line of his stubble.

Their eyes connected as their breathing grew louder. His eyebrows furrowed, and he searched for something in her gaze. Her lips parted.

Remembering how skittish he'd been after they'd kissed earlier, she thought she'd better take this slow, ask his permission before she acted on her desires. 'Is it alright if I make love to you now?'

He gulped and nodded. Removing her hand from his face, she pushed herself onto her knees and swung her leg over his lap. She shook her mane of hair behind her and cupped his jaw between her hands. Leaning over, she kissed him tenderly on his scar, repeating it on the other side. Next, the top of his cheekbones, his nose, his ear, his neck.

His fingers sank into her hips, pulling her down where she felt him growing hard.

'Gabriel,' she gasped. 'Let me take some of your pain away.'

She pressed her lips to his. At the same time she leaned back to lie down, pulling his body with her, so that his weight lay on top of her. She had been right; this sofa was a great place to make out.

His kisses grew more feverish and his mouth travelled towards her ear, down her neck and down to her breast. He took her nipple between his teeth through the fabric of her shirt and bit down gently. She groaned and bucked against him.

Then he stopped. 'I can't do this.'

In the space of a second, the weight of him disappeared and she was left on the sofa, alone. Gabriel paced the room.

'Gabriel...?'

His hands fixed onto his hips. 'This is too dangerous...'

Jess couldn't get her head around what was happening. 'Dangerous...we're just two people taking solace in each other's bodies. It's just *sex*.' Her words seemed to echo in the room and he stopped pacing, his eyes finding hers and pinning her down.

'Is it?'

They stared at each for a beat. What did he mean by that? Her heart thumped painfully.

And then he whipped around on his heel and fled the room.

'Gabriel! Gabriel!' Jess called after him.

But he was gone.

12

At the very top of the stairs, Jess saw two doors illuminated by the dim orange glow of the hallway lights: one closed and one open at the end of the hall. She chose the open one and found herself in a grand bedroom, a four-poster bed dominating the space, the walls painted a tasteful warm grey, and her suitcase waiting for her next to the refurbished, antique wardrobe.

Jess grunted with displeasure and plopped onto her bed, sinking into the feather duvet. What had just happened downstairs? Had she read the situation between her and Gabriel all wrong? What had caused him to push her away?

She stood up and paced the room, the floorboards creaking under her feet. She didn't care if he heard her. Let him! He was being ridiculous. The attraction between them was so sizzling hot that it would warm an entire colony of penguins and yet, he'd just run away from her like she had a disease. Why had he brought her out to his chateau if not to seduce her?

Nope. She wasn't having this. It had taken her a while to come around to the idea of sleeping with a man she hadn't been dating since birth, but now that she had arrived, she wanted it. Her body thrummed with pent-up desire, robbing her of any thoughts of sleep, especially knowing he was just down the hall.

Generally, she didn't swear, but what the actual fuck.

Why was he hiding from her? All she wanted was to give him pleasure and take some in return, right? The only reason it would become a problem is if feelings became involved...

She came to a sudden stop.

'Is it?' She remembered his face when he said those words to her, his eyes haunted.

He's trying to protect himself. She slapped her forehead.

Jess used to think Fatima was the one holding him back, and she was...in a way. He had lost so much when he lost her: his friend, his foot, his sense of security, his joy for life. Elodie's words echoed in her head: *'He's just biding time until he dies.'*

It dawned on Jess that Gabriel had cut himself off from real emotion for so long, he'd forgotten what it felt like to want somebody like he wanted her. If it was half as much as she craved him, then of course he was struggling. This connection between them...it was powerful. Heady. Intoxicating.

But it was also invigorating. It reminded her of the richness and pleasure of life in a primal, natural way.

How could she show him there was still so much to live for?

Jess's eyes migrated to her suitcase and she strode to it, flipping it open. Tucked into a discreet tote bag was some expensive lingerie she'd bought from *Oh! Paulina* in expectation of wearing it for Krish.

She stroked the bag as a plan formed in her head. She'd show him just how much she'd bloomed since she met him, how he didn't have to keep his walls up around her, how they could find solace in each other.

Jess had just the thing to zap him back to life.

GABRIEL STARED at this reflection in the bathroom mirror, his hands leaning on the marble countertop. What was he doing? He'd brought a beautiful woman who wanted to have sex with him to his chateau in the country…and he'd run away from her.

If his penis were a giant club, it would smack him over the head.

What was wrong with him?

It's because you're scared, asshole.

'No, I'm not,' he said out loud.

She's gotten under your skin.

He ran his fingers through his hair and clasped them together at the back of his head. Memories of Jess played through his mind: her smile, her laugh, the scent of her hair, the way-too-comfortable fit of her hand in his. Shame rushed over him when he remembered how he'd left her downstairs. She didn't deserve to be treated badly. She'd had enough of that from her ex.

This isn't just about sex anymore.

'Fuck.' He smacked the counter with his palm and swore again due to the sting. In just a few days, she'd undone eight years of carefully crafted self-control. Somehow she'd diffused his internal security system. He'd thought that, because of her short stay in France and the fact that she'd just broken up with somebody, she wasn't a risk.

Instead, she was the biggest risk of them all.

He hadn't told anybody except his therapist about his trauma in Afghanistan, but something compelled him to tell her. The way she looked at him with those large blue eyes made him want to open his soul to her.

And his heart.

He growled.

What if you just let go?

For years, he'd told himself that he didn't need anybody. He could live his life alone because he'd be a burden to another person. He could survive without love. He'd become adept at filling his time with activities that nourished his mind and kept him engaged, without anyone expecting anything from him.

Then Jess came along with her spontaneity science fair project and made him want to be spontaneous, too. She kindled a dangerous desire to want more for himself—the first crack in his carefully constructed walls. He detected the mortar crumbling, and he hadn't even slept with her yet.

Yet.

He exhaled. Maybe he could sleep with her and still keep his distance. He needed her now, in this moment. Why not allow himself some grace? Just for a couple days. Then she'd go back to her life, and he could go back to his. He just needed to get this out of his system. Fill up his well.

Gabriel slapped the countertop with both hands and dragged his eyes back to his tortured reflection. Who was he kidding? If he walked through that door and went to her, he'd just be making life harder for himself when they had to say goodbye.

Leaning his forehead on the mirror, he closed his eyes.

What should I do?

JESS ADMIRED the final effect of her *Oh, Paulina!* spending spree in the full-length mirror. Krish's loss was Gabriel's gain. She looked HOT.

She'd never worn garters before. It took her a few goes to fasten them to the tops of her stockings, but she'd gotten there in the end.

The light pink balcony bra cradled her breasts, pushing them up. The line of the cup cut halfway through her nipples. Her boobs redefined pert.

The suspender belt cinched around her waist and the sheer panties barely counted as clothes. She even had sleek satin mules to go with the outfit.

After flipping her curls back and forth a few times to fluff up her mane, she narrowed her eyes at the door. *Ready or not, Gabriel Severin, here I come.*

Throwing her shoulders back, she did her best supermodel walk towards the closed door, to give herself confidence. She gripped the handle and threw it open.

Gabriel was standing in the hallway, his fist poised to knock.

'Look, I'm sorry—' he started before his mouth fell open and his intense gaze travelled up and down her body, taking her in. 'Holy Mother of God,' he said.

Getting over his shock, he stepped towards her at the same time as Jess grabbed him by the shirt and pulled him in. Lips crashed together, mouths desperate to taste each other. His hands gripped her at the waist, thumbs kneading her lower ribs. She already felt the thick edge of him pressing into her lower belly. He was the perfect height for her. At just a few inches taller, their frames fit together like a jigsaw. She thought her body had been thrumming before; now she positively vibrated with need. She tugged at his shirt and drew it up, over his head, exposing his hard, sculpted abs to her hungry gaze.

If it were up to her, they'd go straight for the main event, but Gabriel had other ideas. His hand left her waist to slam the door closed behind him, then he twirled her around so she faced the wall. With her palms pressing against the plaster, she ground her bottom into him and he groaned.

'Spread your legs wider,' he commanded.

She did as requested, being careful not to kick his foot by accident. She didn't want him to lose his balance at this delicate, delectable time.

Gabriel lifted her hair away to nuzzle her neck. His left hand roamed around her body to her breast, pressing up over the sensitive skin, but his other hand…oh, his other hand snuck around her right hip and toyed with the upper edge of her panties, just below her belly button. Her stomach fluttered. First one, then another finger slid past the elastic and dipped to the most sensitive part of her. She bit her lip as he rubbed once, twice and then slipped inside her wet centre.

Jess had never been so turned on in her life. What was it about this dark and complicated man that got her so worked up? After their talk that evening, she understood him so much better. This man, who had suffered so much…she wanted nothing more than to bring him joy.

Like the joy he was presently giving to her.

A feeling like a wave about to crash built inside her core. Unexpected release reverberated through her, making it hard to stand. She let her head fall back onto his shoulder, screaming with pleasure. Gabriel knew exactly how to touch her, playing her body like his own personal violin. He kissed her on the temple and she closed her eyes, enjoying the moment.

After catching her breath, she turned without losing contact with him. She wrapped her arms around his neck and said, 'Now it's your turn. Did you bring a condom?'

'Yes,' he said, his voice rough.

She held out her hand. He took the item out of his pocket and placed it on her palm. 'Right. Now I'm in charge. Take your clothes off and get on the bed.'

'Yes, ma'am.' He sat on the edge of the mattress and removed first his shorts, then his boxer briefs, then his prosthesis, propping it up against the bedside table.

'Now lay down,' she ordered him. She was enjoying this new role. She'd never, ever been this domineering in the bedroom. Her underwear acted like armour—the uniform of her sexual awakening.

And she liked it.

If she had a pen and paper, she imagined she could write some pretty sexy poetry right now even though she had no talent for it. At the very least, a deliciously dirty limerick.

While he watched her, she unsnapped the garters and rolled the stockings down her leg. Next she inched the panties off, so excruciatingly slowly that poor Gabriel actually moaned.

'If I'm not inside you within the next minute, I'm going to explode,' he said. She enjoyed the way his eyes swallowed her whole.

'Quiet!' she replied in her best teacherly voice. 'Please and thank you are still magic words, Severin.' Something was raised, but it sure wasn't his hand. He reminded her of a classical painting or a statue, sculpted and toned. Naked Renaissance Man *cum* delicious buffet that she was about to plunder.

'Please, ma'am,' he said again with a sexy half-smile.

'That's better.'

She reached behind her back and took off her bra, tossing it over her shoulder. The suspender belt followed.

'You're a goddess,' said Gabriel, in awe.

Bunching her hair and moving it over one shoulder, she crawled onto the bed and straddled him, reaching for the condom and sliding it onto him. His hands gripped her thighs, pressing into her skin. Holding the base of him between her fingers, she leaned over and kissed his lips. As their tongues danced, she guided him into her, stretching her open. She gasped. The pleasure was immediate and fierce, which was new for her. He just fit.

Their bodies rocked together, separating and returning to each other with increasing urgency. She hadn't wanted to tell him this before they'd had sex—because she didn't want to give him unrealistic goals—but she'd never actually orgasmed during intercourse. Not with Krish, nor with the handful of boyfriends before him. It always happened either manually or orally before or after the event. She'd always assumed she was wired wrong.

But right from the beginning, this felt different. Intensity built inside her, and she sensed herself approaching a tipping point.

'Oh my god, I think I'm going to...' she said, her voice full of wonder as she rested her weight on her arms, letting her take him deeper into her.

'Me, too,' he panted.

And then they did. Her body shuddered in ecstasy. Moments later, he called out her name. She stilled for a moment, luxuriating in all the delicious sensations. Aftershocks ran through her.

Collapsing onto him, their breathing calmed and she laughed. 'That was, um...'

'*Incroyable*,' he provided. She agreed. What they had just accomplished was much better described in French.

She pushed herself up and caught his gaze with hers, brown, warm and still hungry. The connection between them made her want to share just how special this had been for her. She bit her lip, hoping he wouldn't think she was naive or inexperienced. 'You know, I've never, um...*done that* during intercourse before.'

'Done what?'

Jess made an exploding motion with her hand.

'You mean, orgasmed?' he said, his eyes wide with shock, quickly replaced by pride. 'Well, it's a good thing I came along then.' He hooked his hand behind her neck and pulled her down for a kiss.

She noticed how their kisses had changed since that first night they hooked up. Then, they had been the kisses of strangers: physical and passionate, but impersonal. Now she knew *who* she was kissing, they held more tenderness, more sensuality, more awe.

I could get used to this, she thought and smiled.

He took a tissue off the bedside table and disposed of the condom. Jess settled next to him, her leg thrown over his body. As she cuddled into his side, the gentle night air blew through the open window, cooling them off. His hand stroked her skin at the base of her back.

If anyone had asked her if she'd ever feel this way again four days ago, she'd have laughed. But here she was: content and safe in the arms of a good man.

'What are you thinking about?' Gabriel asked her.

She sighed. 'My ex-boyfriend.'

He chuckled. 'Great. Just what every man wants to hear after making love to a beautiful woman.' She liked that he didn't react with jealousy.

'No, not like that.' She swatted his chest. 'I mean, I'm just wondering if it was actually lucky that we split up. We got along really well, but there were always differences between us. Small things, I thought…but maybe they weren't so small. And we were always so focused on the next step. Like, our life stories had already been written and we were just going through the motions. We'd get married. Have kids. Move to Surrey or closer to my parents. Get a dog. I guess it felt like we were ticking off boxes. I never realised that other options existed.'

'Of course, there are always other options.' He twirled a lock of her hair around his finger.

Jess turned her nose towards his skin, breathing him in. 'Yeah, but I didn't know that. For example, I often wonder if I'd still be a teacher if I had known that being an interior designer was an option. Don't laugh! I just didn't know. My parents never talked about jobs like that, it was always: accountant, teacher, lawyer, doctor, nurse, dentist. It never occurred to me that people decorated other people's houses for a living. I'm completely aware of how stupid that sounds, but I just didn't realise that was a job. I mean, don't get me wrong, I love teaching too, but there were other things I could have done…if I'd known.'

'There still are other things you could do.'

She puffed out her lips and turned onto her back. 'Hmmm. I'm not sure I'm built like that. My family is allergic to change.'

Pushing himself onto his elbow, he edged onto his side and asked, 'How so?' His fingers stroked the skin around her belly. She liked how they couldn't stop touching each other. She was finding it difficult to concentrate on their conversation.

'Um, well, we've lived in the same house since I was born and my parents lived in it ten years prior to having me.'

'Okay…'

'My dad has been wearing the same suit for almost 40 years.'

'Sounds very eco-friendly…' He leaned down and kissed her on the shoulder.

'I can see you're not convinced. How's this: every time one of our pet cats dies, my mother has it cremated and the ashes stored in a little cat-shaped urn. Then she uses the urns as bookends and door stops. In our house, it's not what's holding the door open, but who. She just can't handle the idea of the cats not being around anymore.'

'Okay, I'm convinced. That's…certifiable.'

'Actually, you'd love her. She's kind, and a great cook…although don't mention the helicopter thing. It would give her a heart attack.' She giggled, imagining her parents' expressions if they found out.

She glanced at Gabriel, expecting him to laugh, too, but his face had turned serious, his lips pressed in a firm line and his eyes, distant. It only took her a moment to realise her mistake. She'd been talking as though this wasn't a fling, like he'd be meeting her mother in the near future.

You idiot, she reprimanded herself. Of course, they'd never meet. This interlude wasn't for keeps; it was a moment out of time. A holiday from her real life. Back home awaited explanations to her friends and rebuilding her life without Krish, figuring out what to do next.

Unfortunately, her future probably didn't include Gabriel.

The thought made her chest tighten with unanticipated grief.

13

Somewhere outside, a rooster cock-a-doodle-dooed. Or *coco-rico*, as they said in France. Jess recalled teaching her kids about what animals sounded like in other countries and, for a moment, her stomach plummeted at the thought of returning to school soon—a feeling that concerned her. *Remember this is just a hook up. Your life is in London,* she berated herself. *Just enjoy the experience.*

And what an experience it was.

A smile tugged at her lips. She was in a French chateau with an amazing man. Her body ached in all the right places. If this were a book, it would be called *The Sexual Awakening of Jessica Smith* and there would be lots of analogies about ripening fruit.

The bed next to her dipped and she cracked open an eye to find Gabriel reattaching his prosthesis. 'Morning,' she said, reaching out to run her hand along his spine.

'Hey, go back to sleep.' He twisted towards her, leaned down and kissed her on the lips. 'I'm just going to do some yoga outside.'

Yoga! Jess loved yoga. She threw the covers off and bounded out of bed. 'Well, if you don't mind company and you have another mat...' She reached her arms in the air, arching her back like a happy cat, and his eyes roamed hungrily up and down her naked body.

'Fuck yoga,' he said, striding around the bed and pulling her to him. He nibbled on her neck and Jess felt his erection ready for action.

Much as she wanted to do that, too, they had all day and the idea of sunrise yoga appealed to her. Another new experience. Besides, she needed a good stretch after their workouts last night, and she hadn't done any of her normal exercise since arriving in France. After, they could have more sex.

'Uh, uh, uh,' she said, wagging her finger and pulling firmly away. 'Discipline, *mon chérie*. Yoga first.'

'Yes, ma'am.' He saluted.

This dynamic was becoming a thing for them and she was enjoying every second.

At the back of the chateau, she followed him down the short stairs onto a patch of green, dewy grass. The sun peeked over the horizon to her right, softly illuminating the landscape. The temperature was cool, but not uncomfortably chilly.

The chateau's garden stretched as far as her eye could see, a tangle of weeds and shrubs and crumbling stone sheds that abutted the distant tree-line of the forest. In her head, she imagined this land transformed one day: profusions of colourful dahlias, a fruit orchard, vegetable patches, and a gazebo with beanbags for curling up with a good book on lazy, sunny afternoons. For a moment, the vision was so real that it replaced the evidence before her eyes. She shook her head and the mirage faded away.

Gabriel handed her a yoga mat and spread out a towel for himself. He wore only a pair of black boxer briefs. The most yoga-friendly clothing she had was a bra and the bottoms from her camisole set. The cool morning air made her skin goosebump all over, her nipples clearly hardening through the thin fabric.

'I don't know how I'm supposed to concentrate with you looking like that,' he growled.

She just smiled. She knew exactly how he felt. As he moved into his first flows, her eyes swept over his chiselled torso and muscular thighs. She wondered if his prosthetic limb would affect his balance.

When some people say they 'do yoga', what they mean is that they perform a series of gentle, relaxing poses and lie down with their eyes closed a lot. Neither of them subscribed to that. Jess was heartened to see that Gabriel practised the same kind of yoga as her: the kind where he held the forms until his body shook, muscles flexing, pushing himself to his limits.

'You know,' he said as he watched her complete her *chataranga*. 'This is giving me some excellent ideas for positions we could try later.'

She laughed at the same time as a jolt of anticipation shot up her middle. 'Down, dog,' she joked.

Eventually, she fell into sync with his programme, flowing from warrior two into reverse warrior, into side angle down into a plank.

Looking at her with a wicked twinkle in his eyes, he challenged her, 'Bet I can hold a plank longer than you.'

'You're on.'

After glancing at her watch and marking the time, she closed her eyes and concentrated on her breathing, expanding her ribcage to maximum capacity and then letting the air trickle out through her nose. She focused her attention on the titter of birdsong floating through the air.

Five minutes in, Gabriel grunted.

'How you holding up?' she asked breezily. She checked her watch again. Perhaps she should have mentioned that she'd recently completed a plank challenge where she held the position for ten minutes a day. 'All okay?'

'Mm-hmm.' Out of the corner of her eye, she perceived him shaking with exertion.

Finally, he succumbed, collapsing onto the ground. 'Ugh! I give up.'

She lowered herself to the mat in a controlled manner, even though her own muscles burned, and rolled onto her side with a wide grin on her face. 'So what do I win?'

Gabriel spent the next thirty minutes giving her the prize.

WHEN GABRIEL BOUGHT this secluded chateau, the last thing on his mind had been what a perfect place it would be to lay naked in the backyard with a beautiful woman, the sun drying the sweat of exertion on their sated bodies.

Yet, here they were.

This had to be his idea of heaven.

They both lay on his towel, the yoga mat rolled up as a pillow and one of Jess's long legs thrown carelessly over him like they didn't have any worries in the world.

He could get used to this.

Tomorrow, they would head back to Paris. Thursday, Jess would return to London, and he'd return to his old life. His heart clenched and for a beat he forgot to breathe.

Stop thinking about anything past today, warned his inner voice. *Just enjoy this.*

As someone who spent most of his time reliving the past, he found this easier said than done. In the six years he spent in therapy, his psychiatrist, a calm-voiced *Armée de Terre* veteran, had spent most of his time trying to drag Gabriel out of the past, to convince him to think more about the now and worry less about the future.

He'd stopped going two years ago when his therapist suggested Gabriel should start dating again.

He pushed the memory away.

Reaching down, he scratched an itch on his stump. At some point he had kicked off his prosthesis, his sock, and the gel sleeve. Funny... when he was wearing it, his prosthesis felt as much a part of him as any other part of his body, but when it was sitting next to him, like it was now, it mutated into just an object. A tool.

Jess shifted her head onto his shoulder. Her fingers brushed down his stomach, towards his groin. He knew where she was headed.

'Do you mind if I...'

He raised his eyebrow.

'...if I touch your stump?'

Oh. Well, maybe he didn't know. 'Be my guest.' He wasn't ashamed of it; however, he'd never encouraged a sexual partner to lay hands on it before. It seemed too intimate for a one-night stand. But with Jess—well, she could touch any part of him she wanted.

She flipped herself around so that her head lay near his calf. It gave him a beautiful view, right up the plane of her flat stomach to her perfect, round breasts. They reminded him of his old X-Men comics; the female characters like the Phoenix, Storm and Rogue always had amazing boobs, very titillating for his young pre-pubescent brain. He never thought real women looked like that. But the sight of Jess's body could cause traffic accidents.

Not only that, but she was also smart, kind, and funny. A quadruple threat.

Tentatively she ran her fingers over his scar and he shivered.

'Is that okay?' she asked, drawing her hand away.

'It's fine.' He could barely feel it. In the period when he lived with his parents—another hell he never wanted to repeat with his father's amateur therapy attempts and his mother's constant weeping—he had worked hard to desensitise the skin on his stump to ready himself for the prosthetic limb. Next he'd tested a series of different sockets to find one that didn't chafe or cause blisters. Eight years on and it was numb most of the time. But visualisation was powerful, especially for amputees, and just the fact that he saw her touching him made him react.

'It's so much softer than I expected it to be,' she said.

'Well, I moisturise.' It was important to keep the skin in good condition to prevent folliculitis.

'Does it still hurt?'

'Sometimes.' He put his hands behind his head. 'It gets sore. I massage it at the end of every day, usually when I'm cleaning it. Once in a while I get phantom pain out of the blue. Like my brain gets amnesia and suddenly thinks to itself, "Hey, I haven't spoken with Right Foot in a while. Better check in"—and fires off some messages. After five or six hours it usually stops, but fuck me if it doesn't hurt in the meantime. Like lightening under my skin.'

'Did it take you a long time to get used to the prosthesis?'

His mind zipped back to the hours of physical therapy with a Thor-like Austrian named Wolfgang. The man had been like a drill sergeant. 'It took me a while to learn to trust it, to gain confidence that this flimsy bit of metal and plastic would hold my weight. But I managed it in the end.' He'd been a model student, his goal to live on his own again as quickly as possible.

She kissed the puckered line where the doctors had sewn it closed. 'Do you...do you miss your foot?'

This was a question he pondered many times while lying alone in his bed at night, staring at the ceiling and playing sliding doors in his head. If he closed his eyes, he could still identify exactly where his foot should be. But in a way, the missing foot served as a reminder of Fatima, keeping her alive for him. 'In a perfect life, I'd rather have my foot, but I don't let it hold me back. There are very few things that I can't do now that I could do then. I still run. Hike. Cycle. I've bought the best prostheses I can afford and they're making advances all the time. Really amazing advances, actually.'

Blue eyes shining with awe, she said, 'Gosh, you're such an insp—'

'Do NOT say inspiration!' He laughed and swatted her on the leg. 'We call it *inspiration bombing*. Amputees get it all the time. I'll be out on a run and some stranger will come up to me while I'm having a water break and say, "Man, you're such an inspiration" like I just solved world hunger. It makes me want to explode. I'm not an inspiration; I'm just a guy trying to get through life, same as anyone else.'

'I'm so sorry!' She spun around again and laid next to him. 'You'll have to punish me later.' Biting her lip, she flashed his new favourite, flirtatious look—the one where she dropped her chin towards her chest and her eyes devoured him from under her lashes. He loved how far they'd come since the first night when they met. In his opinion, her science fair project won Best in Show.

She laid her head on his chest and they lapsed into a companionable silence. As he stroked her silky hair, feeling the early morning sunshine on his skin and listening to the birds sing and the insects buzz, an alien feeling overcame him. It made him want to smile and dance and buy sweets for children and adopt stray cats. The world seemed a little brighter, the air a little sweeter. With a start, Gabriel realised that, for the first time in a long time, he was happy.

He frowned.

Bolting upright and startling Jess in the process, he reached for his sleeve and slid it onto his stump, followed by the sock.

'Is everything okay?' Concern laced her voice as she pushed herself up.

'Yeah. Uh—do you mind if I go for a quick run?' He needed to move. He needed to sort out his head, to put some distance between himself and this siren for a few minutes so he could regain perspective. Remember that this was a short-term deal.

Thankfully, she didn't seem to detect his panic. 'I wish I'd brought my running gear. I'd've come with you.' She picked up her bra and threaded her arms through the straps.

'You're a runner?' Of course, she was. *Fuck, she might just be the perfect woman.*

'Yup. But you go ahead. I'll have a shower. Get some breakfast ready.'

'Great. Thanks.' He rolled onto all fours, pushed himself up to standing, and escaped into the house, forcing himself not to look back. He had some thinking to do.

14

'I FIND THIS LOOK EXTREMELY SEXY,' JESS SAID. HER CURLS STILL WET
from the shower, she tucked them behind her ears as she surveyed
Gabriel post-run at the bottom of the stairs. His tan skin shimmered
with sweat. A well-loved, navy Yankees baseball cap covered his
damp hair; he wore running shorts and no shirt, which left his
sculpted chest on view; and he'd changed his prosthesis to a futur-
istic blade. What was it about this man that made her feel constantly
frisky?

'I have no problem with that.' Grinning, he swiped off his hat and
ran his arm across his forehead.

She was glad he had returned and seemed to be back to himself.
Before he left, she'd noticed his slight wobble; she chalked it up to
the fact that he wasn't used to spending so much time with another
person, being a 'hermit' as Elodie had called him. Jess had no
problem giving him the space he needed, even though she missed
him for the forty-five minutes he'd disappeared for his run.

Craving him, Jess sashayed over. 'You know what you are?' She
pursed her lips to stop from laughing.

'Don't say it.'

Running a finger down his chest, she said, 'Okay, I won't say it, but you *are* inspiring me...to want to do very naughty things to you.'

He gave her a dangerous look. 'Later. First, a shower. Then, we're going to demolish some shit.'

'I love it when you talk dirty to me,' she joked.

An hour later, she wore protective eyeglasses and a hard hat with her hair tied back, and faced a false wall that needed to disappear. Jess could not be happier. After all the renovation programmes she'd watched, to be standing in a real chateau, about to punch holes in a wall...well, it was a dream come true. While she worked on that job, Gabriel would chip away at an old fireplace across the room. 'I've given you the fun job,' he said.

'I've never demolished anything before! Do I just...?' She made a swinging motion, like hitting a golf ball.

'Not quite.' He demonstrated the correct action with the sledge-hammer and then passed it over to her. 'Just make sure to slide your upper hand down—'

'Like this?' she asked as she swung with all her might and planted the metal head in the wall. It stuck there.

'Yup. Pretty much,' he said, scratching at his hair with a look that said he already regretted putting a weapon of destruction in her hands.

She jumped up and down with glee. 'That was awesome! Wait! You know what we need? Mood music!'

'Good idea. Holst? The Planets?'

'I was thinking AC/DC.'

He groaned.

Jess reached around to the back of her jean shorts and retrieved her phone. 'Gabriel, we have to do something about your taste in music. I just don't get your obsession with classical.'

'It relaxes me,' he said, appearing very unrelaxed. She saw a shadow of grumpy Gabriel in the furrow of his brow.

'Like demolition, you need to choose the right tool for the job. And I'm afraid right now, we need heavy metal.' Scrolling through Spotify, she found a suitable playlist. She hit the triangle, bit her bottom lip, and banged her head up and down as the electric guitar of 'Thunderstruck' bounced between two notes and raced towards that first drum beat. 'Thunder!' she chanted along with the band. Gabriel rolled his eyes, even as the corner of his lip pulled upwards.

Jess braced her leg against the wall and pulled the sledgehammer free. 'Thunder!' She stabilised her legs like she was up to bat at Rounders. 'Thunder!' She heaved the heavy tool back and then slammed it into the wall again, causing a hefty leaf of plaster to crumble away. A surge of power flowed through her. This was fun.

'Yee-hah!' she called out with jubilant abandon.

Gabriel watched her from the other side of the room, arms crossed with a fist covering his mouth, trying to hide his laughter.

She cocked her head at him. 'Come on, Severin. Get to work. I'm not doing it all by myself.'

'Yes, ma'am.' He said, taking a chisel and hammer to the fireplace.

For the next couple of hours, they worked together on their own projects, creating an impressive pile of rubble. Destroying stuff was unexpectedly liberating. With each strike of the hammer, adrenaline flowed through her.

She wasn't imagining that the wall was Krish...but she wasn't *not* imagining that either. Her thoughts turned to last Thursday night. She couldn't believe that it was less than a week ago. She didn't even feel like the same person that he broke up with anymore. Now she was Jess That Had Touched a Cloud; Jess That Had Shagged a Frenchman Senseless and Had an Orgasm During Sex; Jess, Slayer of Chateau Walls with Sledgehammers. If Krish hadn't broken her heart, she never would have had any of those experiences.

She never would have met Gabriel.

The thought made her hit the wall extra hard.

If she didn't know better, she might think that she was *in love*. She barked a laugh and shook the sledgehammer free of plaster before slamming it into the wall again.

That's ridiculous. No way that she could fall out of love with one man and into love with another in the space of four days. That just didn't happen. Not in real life.

And yet...

She rested the sledgehammer on the floor and reached for her water bottle. As she wet her parched throat, her eyes wandered towards Gabriel, who had already dismantled half the fireplace, saving the bricks to reuse in another part of the house. As if he knew she was studying him, he turned his head and winked at her. She even thought she heard him singing along to 'Smells Like Teen Spirit'. A grin creased her face at seeing him, her chest glowing with warmth.

Thinking back to that day she walked into his gallery, she couldn't believe that she'd thought him stand-offish and arrogant. Now she thought he was one of the best people she'd ever met. She felt comfortable with him, like she could be herself, and express herself physically in a way that would have made her blush a week ago. He made her a better version of Jessica Smith. Wasn't that what love did?

But still, *four days...?*

Maybe Krish had been right to break up with her. Maybe she was too buttoned-up. If Krish had been her Mr Right, wouldn't he have brought out this side of her? This new side that she really liked?

But no: Gabriel had been the one to crack her open and find the jewel inside.

AFTER A LONG DAY of restoring the chateau, Jess reclined on the sofa in the library, freshly showered and drinking red wine. From under her lashes, she watched Gabriel flick through his record collection, sheathed in another one of his provocative linen shirts. *He has really sexy hands*, she thought randomly. She admired the tendons pulling and rolling as his fingers walked over the spines of the vinyls, searching for the perfect one.

She'd miss those hands. A lump arose in her throat. Their time together was rushing by too fast.

He'd been a good sport all day, allowing her to choose the tunes they listened to as they demolished their respective bits of chateau. She had never realised how much joy smashing things with a sledge-hammer would bring her. Her arm muscles ached in a hard-won, satisfying way.

The experiences were coming thick and fast with this man, and she didn't want them to stop.

What if they didn't have to? chirped a rogue voice inside her.

With determination, she closed the door on that line of thought. *It's just a fling*, she reminded herself.

What if it's not?

Jess pursed her lips. How would she even know? How could she tell the difference between steamy sexual attraction to a man who's helping her to recover from heartbreak and real love? Was there a test in *Cosmo* for that?

All she knew was that, when she looked at him, her heart grinned. She wanted nothing more than for him to be happy. When she'd met him, he'd been so serious and closed off. Now, he was humming a song, smiling easier, laughing more. This was the real Gabriel. She hated to think that he might return to the old Gabriel when she left.

If she left.

Don't be ridiculous. She had to go home. She couldn't just uproot herself to find out if this was a rebound relationship or true love.

Why not? What if this could be your life?

For the first time, it occurred to her that the person she fell in love with could shape her life in a way she hadn't previously contemplated. Love derailed the best-laid plans: just look at Grace Kelly and Prince Rainier of Monaco, Wallis Simpson and King Edward VIII, Johnny Cash and June Carter.

Growing up, she'd never considered leaving England or deviating from her primary school teacher, two-up-two-down house in the country, two kids, husband and dog fantasy. But now, a new possibility was forming in her heart. One centred around life in Paris, where she taught at a bilingual school—which, again, she hadn't even realised was a thing until Elodie showed her. She and Gabriel would renovate their chateau on weekends, documenting it on YouTube, and eventually moving there or turning it into a bed-and-breakfast or just throwing amazing parties for their new, yet-to-be-acquired friend group. She'd learn French past the secondary school level and how to tell the difference between chardonnay and sauvignon.

Then again, she might be living in cloud cuckoo land. She knew Gabriel felt something for her—of that she was certain. But was it pick-up-your-life-and-relocate-yourself-to-a-new-country-for-me kind of love? Was she brave enough to find out?

'*Voila!*' Gabriel exclaimed, making Jess jump. He pulled a record off the shelf and brandished it in front of her with an excited smirk and a mischievous sparkle in his eyes. Her breath caught.

This man...life would be so much more vibrant with him by my side...

'I'm going to turn you into a classical music lover.'

'You can try.' She laughed nervously, attempting to recover herself. 'I think it's about as likely as turning you into a Spice Girls fan, but—you get a sticker for persistence.'

'I have a feeling you'll like this. It's Beethoven's Pastorale symphony...his sixth.' He placed the vinyl on the turntable and picked up the needle, dropping it delicately onto the grooved black plastic. For a moment nothing happened and then the sound of jaunty violins and deep cellos soared through the air.

She was willing to try anything once, especially for him. The anticipation on his face at the idea of sharing this with her made her feel noticed. Like her enjoying this mattered to him.

Her heart beat a little faster.

Gabriel cradled his red wine glass in his palm and settled next to her on the sofa.

'What's so special about this song?' she asked.

'First of all, he wrote this *song* after he went deaf. Whenever I think something is too hard, I remember Beethoven writing a symphony he could only hear in his head—and it reminds me that nothing is impossible.' His gaze lingered on hers briefly before narrowing and cutting to his wine glass. She wished she could read his mind. Was he thinking about them, too? Did he think they were impossible? Did he want them to be possible?

'Okay, that's pretty impressive,' she said as questions leapfrogged through her head.

He cleared his throat and continued, 'But other than that, this one is all about the great outdoors and man's relationship to nature. More than any other symphony, the sixth paints a picture. Lay back and close your eyes.' She followed his instructions. 'Imagine yourself arriving in the countryside. See the birds in the air; feel the sun on your face. Imagine the farmers working in the fields. Everybody's smiling. Can you see it?'

Amazingly, she could. As the music unfurled, a sense of deep contentment and relaxation flowed through her veins, similar to the peace that hiking outside in a beautiful landscape inspired. She breathed deeply like she stood on a mountaintop. Gabriel's thumb stroked along the back of her hand, further lulling her into a cocoon of tranquility. She could stay here forever.

They remained silent as they listened together. Then as the strings took over, he said, 'Now we're standing near a brook, the water pouring over the rocks...'

'I can hear it.' She grinned, marvelling as the picture formed in her head through the soundscape.

'...The birds are trilling. The flute and oboe are two nightingales, jumping from branch to branch...now the clarinets are a cuckoo bird...'

'This is magical.' She completely saw what he was describing, a forest full of life. Beethoven painted with notes. Disobeying Gabriel's orders for a moment, she cracked open an eye and peeked over at him. He was watching her, an unguarded smile on his face that made her stomach flip.

'Enjoying it so far?' he asked.

She nodded and he leaned towards her ear, whispering, 'Just wait til the end.' A thrill charged through her.

Taking a sip of her wine, she rolled it around her tongue and then laid her head back again, re-closing her eyes.

Gabriel continued describing the next section, the country folk dancing, stamping their feet and making merry. Jess visualised the blue sky, the free-flowing beer, people lounging on hay bales.

'But then, because every good thing must come to an end, a thunderstorm arrives.'

Cymbals crashed and drums beat, the music churning urgent and angry. It sounded just like thunder and lightning and echoed the tempest inside of her. His words reminded her that they'd be leaving here tomorrow. She frowned. Jess wished they could stay in this bubble, avoid real life, even just for another day. The time was passing too fast. Tears formed behind her eyelids, and her breathing became fast and shallow, edged with sadness, caught up in the hectic drive of the symphony.

'But now the sun is coming back out again,' he said and it filled her with relief. Hope.

The music changed, turning calmer and brighter. She didn't need Gabriel to tell her what was happening anymore. The country folk emerged from their houses; the cows called out in the fields; the blue sky reappeared.

'Keep your eyes closed,' Gabriel said as he lifted the wine glass from her hand. She heard the gentle donk of the base hitting the wood as he placed it on the side table.

She did as instructed and listened to the horns and strings tumble over each other in happiness. A rustle of cloth caught her ear as Gabriel shifted his body. She only realised that he was kneeling between her legs when his hands grasped her hips and pulled her down towards him, so that her bottom lined up with the edge of the sofa.

Jess yelped. Eyes still shut, she smiled. 'Gabriel, what are you—?'

'Shhh,' he said. 'Just trust me. Listen. Feel.'

His fingers slipped under the hem of her dress and peeled her underwear slowly down her legs. He pushed the fabric of her skirt up around her waist and the air hit her naked skin. The person she used to be would have hated being on display like this, but with Gabriel, it made her insides dance with anticipation.

'You are exquisite,' he said, as he looped his arms under her legs, pushing her knees up. His breath tickled her inner thigh. She bit her lip, looking forward to what was coming next. Her breathing shallowed. The music grew more urgent, like it was heading towards something big.

His lips touched the most sensitive part of her. Then he licked right up her seam before burying his tongue completely in her, his head nestled deep between her thighs.

Jess sighed. The music filled her head, the notes tumbling over each other in their eagerness to reach the end. In her mind's eye, the country folk danced in an orgy of good fortune. Her hands fisted around the piped edge of the sofa cushion and squeezed. In that moment, life coursed through her, like it did when she was on the helicopter. She was Mother Nature herself. Fertile. Giving. And very, very wet.

She detected her own crescendo building with the music, and the image of the country folk fled her mind, replaced only with thoughts of Gabriel and what he was doing to her. Her hands snaked into his hair.

He concentrated his attention on the place that mattered most.

The symphony crested and broke, the notes undulating and carrying her along. 'Gabriel!' she screamed as ripples of pleasure engulfed her. She practically felt the sunshine on her skin, warm and life-affirming, even though the room was shadowy and lit by the orange glow of one lamp.

Her bones melted as she lay there. Her breathing slowly settled while the horns finished off the symphony. She pulled at Gabriel's arms, wanting to devour him. He replaced her dress over her lap and nibbled up her body until he sat next to her again. With a self-satisfied smirk on his face, he rested his arm on the back cushion and propped his head up on his hand. 'So…how do you feel about classical music now?'

'It's bloody amazing. You're bloody amazing.' She pushed herself into a seated position and threw her leg over his lap, straddling him and pulling his lips to hers. She never did this with Krish after he went south on her, but with Gabriel it felt right, the sweetness of her most private place like a secret between them.

Pulling away, she said breathily, 'Gabriel…?'

'Yes?' He grew still as she gazed into his dark, liquid eyes.

She stroked her thumb along his cheekbone and gave him her most earnest Disney princess stare. 'You really are an inspiration.'

He barked with laughter and they dissolved into fits together, which ended in another frantic kiss. *This moment is perfect,* Jess thought. Here—with this man, on this couch, in this chateau. If time stopped right now, she'd die happy.

But of course time didn't do that. It marched forward. Tomorrow they'd leave here and, the following day, she'd return to London.

Her heart plunged at the thought.

15

MERDE. GABRIEL STARED AT THE CEILING, TOO DEEP IN THOUGHT TO sleep. The light breeze from the open window did nothing to soothe his hot skin. Jess slept deeply beside him.

He wanted to put a pin in time, give himself longer to figure things out.

She had turned his world upside down. In just a few days, Jess had burrowed into his life and knocked down all his walls, like a bomb. What was it about this specific woman that made it hard to breathe when she wasn't sharing his air?

You're turning into a poet, scoffed his inner asshole.

Shut up.

He didn't understand what was happening to him. His experience of relationships with the opposite sex would fill a Post-It note. Sure, he'd had some girlfriends in college, but nothing to write home about. And then when his career as a war photographer took off, he quickly realised his work wasn't conducive to commitment. Even though Fatima had a wife back home, he personally thought it was cruel to put a partner through the worry of being chained to a war photographer. The job was just too unpredictable and there were long stretches where he couldn't communicate with home. He already felt guilty enough putting his parents and Elodie through it. He didn't want that list any longer than it needed to be.

Besides, he was chasing stories, not love. He always supposed there'd be time for that, later, so he sealed his emotions away.

Instead, he had sex. No strings. Wherever he had assignments. Journalists, other photographers, embassy staff. Fatima used to call his assignations 'F-Stops' or Fuck-Stops—a reference to the photography term for the size of the opening in a lens.

But with Jess, the sex wasn't about slaking a thirst of his body. It was about feeding the needs of his soul.

Seriously, this is some byronic-level shit, said that annoying voice again.

Fuck it. Okay. So Jess brought out his poetic side.

It's okay, you know. You aren't betraying anybody by falling in love.

He huffed cynically and then checked to make sure he hadn't woken Jess up. Love? Not possible. He'd only known the woman for less than a week. How could this be love? Surely, love didn't happen with a bang, like in the movies. Real love—the kind that lasted—formed over time, didn't it? And time was the one thing they didn't have.

Then again, the thought of her leaving tomorrow hollowed him out inside. The very idea of her going back to London and getting on with her life, meeting somebody else to make her laugh, wrapping her legs around a man that wasn't him…it made his mouth taste bitter and his stomach tighten in a knot.

Gabriel realised he had the top sheet clenched in his fist. He released it.

He wanted to be the one she took risks with. *He* wanted to be the one to make her laugh. *He* wanted to be the first person she called when she had good news to share.

But was he still capable of being that guy? Up until now, he believed that part of him had died in the hills of Afghanistan. He used to think he was brave, running headfirst into war zones, but right now he felt like the world's biggest coward. Should he follow Jess's lead and take some risks?

If a person can die in a split second, then you can decide to live in the same timeframe.

Ha! Now who's the poet? accused Gabriel, scowling.

As though sensing his stress, Jess snorted in her sleep and murmured what sounded like *Pickles*. An involuntary grin ripped across his face. Even asleep, she made him smile.

How could he let her go?

How could he *not*?

The grin slipped from his lips, which resumed their habitual downturned position. Her life was back in London. She had friends, a family, a job. His desire to keep her here was selfish. What did he have to offer her?

There was a reason he'd avoided relationships for the past eight years. Life was safer if the only person he had to worry about was himself. He'd built a good life, a quiet life—alone. He had plenty to nourish his soul: his plants, his music, his work, his pottery, his exercise, his chateau—

Although how could he ever come here again and not bathe in her memory? In two days, she'd infused these walls with her presence.

'Bathe in her memory'? laughed the voice. *You're such a douche. You've got it bad.*

Fuck. I know, he admitted, squeezing his eyes closed. He raised his hands to his face and rubbed his forehead. He had to get this woman out of his system.

Gabriel rolled onto his side and observed the shadowy curves of her sleeping form.

This whole tortured monologue was probably redundant

anyway. Jess didn't come to Paris looking for a man to replace the one who had just broken her heart. She came ready for a good time. *Une aventure.* He was just an experiment in her spontaneity science fair project. Exhibit A. Besides, her bucket list most likely didn't include falling in love with an ex-war photographer with a high heap of baggage and a missing foot.

For all he knew, she still pictured her ex when she and Gabriel had sex—even though, from the way she called out his name, he doubted it. And the fact that she orgasmed with him during inter-course made him want to crow like a cockerel. *'Coco-rico! I'm king of the world.'* He was so proud, he might add it to his résumé under 'Skills'.

Again, he wished that this night would never end.

He was hard again. Jess had turned him into a human tent pole. Now that they were racing against the clock, he needed more of her. He wanted to stretch this night into an eternity. Moving closer to her body, he glided his hand over her lower belly. An invitation. He waited.

Within seconds, she sleepily responded to him, snaking her hand behind his neck to pull him to her, snuggling her spine into his stomach, and inching her knees wider to give his hand better access.

God damn it, I think I'm in love this woman, he thought with wonder, his heart aching in his chest.

Even if he couldn't have her.

16

'SMILE FOR THE CAMERA!' SAID JESS AS SHE HELD UP HER PHONE TO take a selfie of them together. She and Gabriel were picnicking on the grass out back, their final lunch before returning to Paris. An hour ago, she'd realised that she hadn't taken any photos of their time at the chateau, and now she was making up for it.

She checked the photo and saw that Gabriel had not followed her instructions. 'That's not a smile, Gabriel.'

'And *that's* not a camera. *This* is a camera.' He pointed with his chin towards his Fuji DSLR, sitting on the blanket beside him.

It seemed that Gabriel had come to the same realisation and also decided he wanted pictures. He'd spent most of their picnic time snapping away at her. Krish used to take pictures of her when they were on holiday together, but with him, she always felt like she was just another pretty element in his image, sharing equal billing with the sunrise or the beach—always composed to perfection. Beautiful shots, but very staged.

The way Gabriel photographed her, she felt like he was trying to capture her soul. The real her. Laughing. Unposed. Just Jess. She liked that. He observed her in a way that Krish never had. Intimately and completely. Like she was the most important thing in the frame.

She elbowed him in the ribs playfully. 'But I want a picture of us both. *And* I want a smile. Let's do it again.'

Jess held up her phone and hit the button. This time when she checked the image, Gabriel was smiling wide…and crossing his eyes.

'Gabriel!'

'I've noticed you like saying my name a lot.'

It was true. She loved how it rolled off her tongue. Three sexy syllables. 'Yes, especially when you're acting like one of my naughty kids…Gabriel!'

He laughed and she turned in his arms, pushing him back onto the grass. With ninja-like moves, she sat on his chest and held the phone above him with one hand, while tickling him under the armpits with the other. She didn't know if the photos would be any good, but they were enjoying the moment.

Finally, he managed to grab her wrists and flip her onto her back. Pinning her down, he kissed her, stealing her breath away and melting her into the grass.

The kiss gradually slowed and then stopped. He hovered above her. His smiles, gone. His eyes, thoughtful. They wandered over her face, like he was memorising details, and they breathed in the scent of each other. Her heart thundered in her chest.

She didn't know what made her say it, but before she could stop herself, the words slipped out of her mouth: 'Gabriel, I think I'm falling in love with you.'

Jess didn't care if she'd only known him since Friday night. A lot had happened in that time. Enough for her to know that he was special, not at all what she had expected, but everything she wanted. Sexy, thoughtful, funny, talented, smart, adventurous…

…and looking at her like she'd just announced she was a bodysnatcher.

'You don't mean that,' Gabriel said. He rolled off of her and sat up, wrapping his arms around his knees and looking away from her towards the tree line.

'But I do.' A rebellious swell of anger reared within her. She knew what she meant. Perhaps it had been a mistake to say it, but she still felt the truth of the words in her heart.

'You wouldn't say that if you knew who I really was.'

'And who is that?' Her flash of anger dissolved and she touched his arm. He jerked away like she'd burned him.

'I'm not good enough for you. You deserve…' He shook his head. 'You're looking for a hero, someone to save you from your heartbreak. I'm not that man.'

'You're one of the best people I've ever met.' This time when she touched his arm, he didn't flinch away.

'You've only just met me.'

'I'm a good judge of character.'

'Are you?' He turned and skewered her with his indignant gaze, and she knew before he said it that she wouldn't like what came out of his mouth next. 'Were you a good judge of character with your ex?'

She caught her breath. That observation struck true, like a knife to her heart. Her brow furrowed, unable to dismiss his point and hurt that he'd made it. She used to think she was good at reading people, but obviously she wasn't. First Krish…now Gabriel. The Gabriel of the past couple days wouldn't have said something so mean to her. Maybe her instincts were off here, too.

'I'm-I'm sorry,' she said. 'You're probably right. I just got carried away in the moment…missing this place already.'

'You said it to me yourself: it's just sex, right?'

'Right.' She remembered saying that to him two days ago, and it had been *him* that questioned it. Now, they'd obviously flipped positions. More fool her.

Not wanting to linger on this conversation, she stood up abruptly, smoothing the wrinkles out of her skirt. 'Well, I guess we should clear this up. Get on our way.'

At least she didn't have to second guess what he was thinking anymore. Now she knew. Loud and clear.

Too bad her heart ached like an iron fist was squeezing it. Emotionally, she had jumped from a tsunami into a typhoon and had no idea how to navigate either.

SHIT, shit, shit.

He'd ruined things with Jess. Why did he have to tear her down when she said she thought she was falling for him? He didn't have to be cruel.

Because you're an unloveable douchebag, said his inner critic.

The other day you wanted me to let go, be free, he reminded himself.

And you did. Now it's time to crawl back into your box. You didn't think you could have this, did you? You aren't relationship material and you'd only disappoint her. She'd leave you eventually, anyway.

Besides, her life was in London. He couldn't ask her to leave her ageing parents, a job she loved, and friends she'd miss. In Paris, she would be in a land where she didn't speak the language, jobless, pining for her family...in return for what? *Him?*

What a shit bargain that would be. He couldn't do that to her.

He shoved the final bag into the trunk of the car and waited for Jess to come out of the chateau. After they'd cleaned up the picnic, she'd excused herself to go to the bathroom. It didn't take a rocket scientist to figure out that she wanted somewhere private to cry.

Gabriel covered his face with his hands and dragged them down until his fingertips rested on his mouth. This weekend she had taken him apart and put him back together. And this was how he repaid her?

He'd make it up to her tonight—show her with his body how he felt, so that he didn't have to tell her with his words. The last thing he wanted was for her to leave angry at him.

Especially when he felt the same way she did.

17

GRADUALLY, THE GREEN COUNTRYSIDE GAVE WAY TO CONCRETE AND the clear highway turned more congested. Jess watched a car inch past them in the right lane, a little girl in a child's seat peering out of the window. Their eyes met across the tarmac. The girl smiled; out of habit, Jess smiled, too, although her heart wasn't in it.

It had become a very quiet car ride.

He'd spent the first hour of the trip asking her questions about teaching and wanting to know about her life in London. She guessed he was trying to make up for what happened back at the chateau. Jess answered him, but the conversation eventually petered out and they both turned introspective.

All she heard in her head was him saying, *It's just sex, right?* Of course it was. How silly of her to have convinced herself that it was anything else. And he was right about her judgment, too. She needed to recalibrate, avoid men for a while.

She pulled at the collar of her dress. Was it possible for the air to be heavier in Paris? The closer they got, the more she felt it pressing against her, telling her to go back. Could Gabriel feel it too? All she knew was that the smile she'd uncovered at the chateau had gone.

Now he looked like a man who was mentally cataloguing the to-do list that he'd run away from in the first place.

The congestion cleared and the traffic sped up again. She tracked a grey Tesla as it flashed by in the fast lane.

Sighing, she tried to engage him again. 'So what do you have planned for the next few days?'

He muttered something about a meeting with his agent tomorrow afternoon and needing to repot some of his plants. He was also running a charity 10k to raise money for children who needed prostheses due to land mines—which did nothing to help the black hole that was opening up in her heart at the thought of walking away from him. He was a good man, even if he couldn't see it.

Trying to keep her emotions off her face, Jess asked, 'Do you have a donations page on Facebook?'

'I'm not on Facebook. Or any social media.'

There went her plan to cyber-stalk him from London, but she wasn't surprised. Gabriel didn't strike her as somebody who would suffer the time-wasting pointlessness of social media.

'Well, let me know where I can donate,' she said before sliding back into her thoughts again.

She imagined her own weekend: changing her Facebook status from 'in a relationship' to 'single', fielding the inevitable barrage of questions in her DMs, unfriending Krish. Maybe Gabriel had the right idea. Maybe she should delete the app.

The idea of going home to her empty flat in Battersea made her shift uncomfortably in her seat. She pictured opening the door and seeing the evidence of the life she used to share with Krish all around her: her bed still covered in the outfits she decided not to bring to Paris; the quaint painting hanging on her wall that he'd bought her in Cornwall on their first holiday together; his toothbrush on her sink.

And because that hadn't been enough heartache for her, she'd also be thinking about the man she'd randomly fallen for on her closure tour of Paris.

Well done, Jess, you idiot, she thought, catching the reflection of her forlorn face in the window. Her sad eyes refocussed and she realised they were passing the girl in the car again. The child smiled a second time and gave Jess a thumbs up, like she suspected Jess needed a boost. Children seemed to have a sixth sense when it came to the moods of the grown-ups around them.

It reminded her that she could count on her kids to cheer her up. In just a couple weeks, they'd be back at school and she wouldn't have time to think about the seriously crap summer she'd had. Nothing like meeting a new class of twenty five-year-olds to keep one occupied.

The girl showed Jess her doll, but then the traffic sped up more and the girl's car fell behind. Gabriel switched on the indicator as their exit approached on the right. Soon, they'd be back in Montmartre.

Unexpectedly, Gabriel slammed on the brakes, throwing her forward against her seatbelt. He swore in French. In what seemed like slow motion, Jess whipped her head around to see a red car careening towards them from the outside lane. She braced for impact, but it miraculously missed them by inches, instead smashing into the car in front of Gabriel's SUV. It then spun into the next lane, narrowly missing the girl's car, before skidding to a stop.

Traffic froze. Trembling, Jess breathed quick and heavy, her hands gripping the door and the central console. Gabriel's arm was pasted across her chest, protecting her.

He undid his seatbelt with visibly shaking hands and reached for her, cradling her head in his palm, his eyes frantic. 'Are you alright?' Panic infused his voice as he scanned her over to check for injuries.

She cupped his face, too, and kissed him. Fast and desperate. 'I'm fine. You?'

'I saw that car swerve and hit the barrier. It happened so fast.' He rested his forehead against hers before retreating to the driver's side. For a moment, he closed his eyes. She squeezed his hand.

Jess watched people filtering out of their cars, approaching the vehicles involved in the crash and placing reflective triangles on the ground. Gabriel opened his eyes and surveyed the scene.

'I'll be right back. You stay here,' he said, reaching behind his seat for his high-vis vest and turning to open the door.

'Gabriel!' she said, reaching for him. He glanced back. The shock of the past minute buzzed through her and the words *I love you* were on the tip of her tongue again, but she wasn't going to make that mistake a second time. Instead, she said, 'Be careful.'

He nodded.

She glued her eyes to him as he approached the crumpled car in front of them. Gabriel yanked the driver's side door open and helped an older man exit. Jess spied blood on his forehead, but he seemed to be walking around okay. In the distance, Jess heard the sound of sirens. The lane of traffic to her left managed to filter through, leaving the other three lanes to deal with the mess. A small, concerned crowd gathered around the red car. Its bodywork appeared to be in bad shape and Jess hoped the driver was okay.

Gabriel continued to care for the other driver: retrieving a blanket from the man's car, spreading it on the ground and getting him to assume the recovery position. Jess's chest swelled with love. She suddenly understood how Lois Lane must have felt when she watched Superman saving things—all the more heroic in this instance because Gabriel must be just as shaken up as she was and yet he was out there, helping. He had told her that she wanted a hero; well, to her, he was one.

Shutting her eyes, she concentrated on quietening the erratic beat of her heart. Blood screamed past her ears. Her body shook with realisation.

They could have died.

If that car had been just a few inches closer, it would have hit the front of their car. Who knows if they would have survived? She had never been in an accident before, so this was another entirely new experience—but unlike the others she'd had on this trip, this one she could have done without.

However, it had clarified one thing for her: life was fragile and short—too short to waste time. Tonight she'd try again with Gabriel. She'd convince him to have a go at dating long-distance, just to see if this was more than a fling. They deserved the chance to find out. As the accident had shown her, life could be snatched away at any moment.

For that reason, she'd take one more risk on this trip.

JESS COULD HAVE DIED.

Gabriel slammed the trunk and hefted his backpack over his shoulder. He'd return to collect the rest of his stuff another time. Right now, he just wanted to go home.

It was almost 8PM. The accident had taken a few hours to clear, and he'd given his name as a witness to the police. He felt angry for the stupid kid driving the red car who might not walk again; he was angry at the randomness of fate; and he was angry at the fact that he'd lost precious time with Jess. This was not how he wanted to spend their last night together.

Perhaps it was the universe reminding him that this wasn't meant to be.

Jess could have died.

Next to him, Jess pulled her bag behind her as they exited the parking garage where he stabled his car. Her other hand sought out his, and they clasped their fingers together, tight.

They didn't have far to walk to his apartment. Just a couple of blocks.

From the way she'd barely spoken since their Near-Death Experience and how she clung to his hand now, he could tell that she was still processing. Gabriel believed that there were two types of people when it came to NDEs: those who reacted well and those who reacted badly. By 'well', he meant that it gave them a new lease on life. They might find religion or feel like they've been saved by a higher power. For some, it refocused them on what was important to them.

In other cases, it went the opposite way. It made the person feel isolated, hopeless.

Jess could have died.

He'd had enough therapy and done enough soul searching in the days after he woke up in a hospital bed in Kabul, that he knew exactly where he fell on the scale. In his short life, he'd had so many NDEs that he could rank them; this one today—definitely at the bottom of the list. That didn't mean it hadn't affected him; physiologically, yes. But psychologically, no. He'd made his peace with death long ago.

She could have died.

But Jess...she wasn't used to this sort of thing. All he wanted to do that night was to take care of her. When they returned to his apartment, he'd order take-out and then draw a hot bath so they could soak out their stresses together, shut out the world with all its pain and injustices.

And tomorrow he would say goodbye.

Jess was worried about Gabriel.

Since the accident, he'd been very quiet. The frown was even more pronounced. He had that look in his eyes that she'd come to recognise in a short time as his internal gaze, the one where he was watching events in his mind, not the ones in front of him.

And now, he was holding her hand so tight that she feared the circulation might get cut off, like he didn't want to let her go.

She needed to take care of him tonight and make sure that he was okay. Maybe she should try to move her return train by a day. The thought of leaving him alone if he had been triggered by the accident didn't sit well with her.

As they approached his building, Jess clocked the restaurant where she'd first met Gabriel, light spilling onto the pavement. It was packed full of hungry customers. She spotted her waiter threading through the tables with his little tray, delivering bottles of wine to the thirsty diners. It reminded her that life went on whether she witnessed it or not. Back in London, Krish was probably kissing Francesca. Her parents were probably watching the nightly news. Her students were probably being tucked into their beds, counting the days until school started again.

'Gabbouche!'

A tall East Asian man sitting at the closest table to them stood and waved his arms in the air like he was landing a plane. He seemed to be looking at them. *Gabbouche?* Did he mean Gabriel? She scrunched her nose.

Next to her, Gabriel stiffened before dropping her hand.

'Jay-bot?' he said, his eyes lighting up. Without a backwards glance, he strode across the pavement towards the visitor, and they threw their arms around each other in a crushing embrace. She had never seen men hug for so long—at least twenty seconds. Finally, they separated and did that double back slap thing that men did. The visitor dropped some cash on the table and picked up a backpack and duffel bag before following Gabriel to the building entrance, where she stood. The man's clothes were crumpled as though he'd been travelling for a long time. Gabriel's frown had been replaced by a huge grin.

She heard the man say in a posh English accent, 'I'm sorry I missed Fatima's birthday this year. I was shooting in Zhongdong and the bus broke down—'

'Don't worry about it. You're here now.' Gabriel patted the man on the back and squeezed his shoulder.

Jess realised who this must be: the third person kidnapped along with Fatima and Gabriel. She couldn't remember his name.

Gabriel passed by her and opened the door to the building, almost like he'd forgotten she was there. With a raised eyebrow aimed at Jess and an intrigued half-smile, the man asked, 'And this is…?'

For a moment, Gabriel closed his eyes and shook his head as though trying to remember her name. She struggled to keep the friendly smile stuck to her face. 'Johnson…this is Jess. Jess, Johnson.'

That was it: Johnson Lee. She remembered now. She spotted the bump halfway up his nose where, according to Gabriel, it had been broken during the kidnapping. Other than that, he had a handsome, open face with a ready smile.

Jess reached out to shake his hand. French people normally greeted each other with a *bise*, but this man was a fellow British citizen. A handshake felt more appropriate. 'Pleasure to meet you,' she said.

'The pleasure is all mine,' said Johnson as he kept hold of her hand and brought it to his lips for a chivalric kiss to her knuckles.

Gabriel glared at him. 'Down, Johnson. This one's mine.' She knew she shouldn't like it—because it was a little bit Neanderthal— but she loved that Gabriel referred to her as *'mine.'* It made her think that maybe there was a chance for them, despite what he'd said earlier. Hope flared in her chest.

Johnson laughed. 'Forgive me. I've been living in a cave for a month, starved of the company of beautiful women.'

She tittered politely because she knew that's what she was supposed to do. But inside, she wasn't in the mood for his flattery. All she wanted was to spend her last evening alone with Gabriel, and now it looked like they would have to share it with this man. Not only that, but surely he would dredge up memories for Gabriel that they'd spent the past few days putting to rest. In addition to how Gabriel had reacted in the aftermath of the car accident, it gave her an uneasy feeling and lodged a stone of worry in her stomach. She hid her concern behind a thin smile.

As they waited for the lift to arrive, Gabriel and Johnson chatted about the assignments that he had been on since they saw each other on Fatima's previous birthday. Some were war zones; some not; some were places Jess had never even heard of before. Listening to him made her feel unworldly. Well, one thing was for certain: he'd definitely been busy. Another photographer married to his work. She squeezed into the lift with them, just managing to get her suitcase across the line.

Gabriel flicked on the lights in his flat and Johnson said, 'Do you mind if I crash on your sofa tonight?'

Jess's eyes widened. The last thing she wanted was for this stranger to listen in on her final night of sex with Gabriel. She'd become much more vocal with him and planned to go full opera singer tonight. No chance she'd have this Lothario eavesdropping.

She turned to Gabriel, speaking up for the first time since his visitor arrived. 'Why doesn't he stay in the rental flat? I can go and clear out my stuff…?'

'Good idea. You'll be more comfortable there,' said Gabriel while he chose a bottle of wine from his rack. *Phew*. At least they were on the same page with that.

'Thank god,' said Johnson, eyeing Gabriel's plant collection. 'Sleeping in here makes me feel like I'm trapped in the Amazon again. Hey, speaking of which, remember that time in Peru, with the girl from the British embassy...'

'...and the green anaconda?' Gabriel added, popping a cork on a bottle of red.

'So, she's stationed in Cairo now. She says hi, by the way.'

Jess didn't miss Johnson's wink or the quick glance that Gabriel threw her way, as though this was a story he didn't want her to hear.

Frankly, she didn't want to hear it either. The uneasy feeling of being a third wheel grew inside her. Maybe they just needed a few minutes without her hanging around. 'I tell you what,' she said, already heading for the door. 'While you two reminisce, I'll go downstairs and sort out the flat.'

'Are you sure?' Gabriel asked.

'It's no problem.' She smiled, glad to be getting away. 'Just tell me where the clean sheets are.'

Gabriel poured wine into three glasses. 'I have no idea. You'll have to ask Elodie.'

'Okay, I'll call her.' Jess already had Elodie's number plugged into her phone from the booking. She escaped into the hallway and leaned against the door for a minute. Without her there, she heard Gabriel and Johnson's muffled, deep voices falling into a comfortable pattern of conversation.

Why did he have to turn up tonight of all nights?

Taking a deep breath, she hit Elodie's contact button on the phone. It only rang once before she picked up.

'*Allo?*'

'Hi, Elodie, it's Jess here.'

Elodie didn't miss a beat. 'Jess! Great to hear from you. Is everything okay?'

'All's well. I just need to know where you keep the clean sheets for the bed in the flat.' Her voice echoed in the empty hallway.

'Hmm. That sounds promising. I take it you're having a good time then?' Jess detected the naughty insinuation in Elodie's voice.

'No...I mean, yes, but I need them because when we returned from Gabriel's chateau—'

'Wait. Gabriel took you to his chateau?'

'Just for a few days.'

'Huh. He hasn't even taken me to his chateau.'

Jess smiled, pleased that it had been as special as she thought. 'It was a real spur-of-the-moment thing.'

'Mm-hmm.'

'*Anyway*, his old friend Johnson Lee was waiting for us—'

'That old letch? He hits on me whenever he comes to visit, like he's going to de-lesbian me. It's become a ritual.' Contrary to her words, Elodie sounded fond of him.

'Well, he wants to stay the night, so I need to change the sheets.'

Elodie snorted. 'I wouldn't bother. You only slept in it for what, two nights?' *One night*, Jess corrected in her head. 'It's not worth the laundry. Besides, he's used to sleeping in much worse, in his line of work.'

'If you're sure...' Her mother would be appalled. If somebody else even touched the guest bed, she'd change it.

'I'm sure. But listen, do me a favour? Don't let them drink too much. A bottle or two is fine, but after that, they both start getting maudlin. Not a good scene.'

Jess blew air out of her lips. 'I'll do my best.' She didn't want Gabriel to get drunk either. Not on her last night.

'Are you still leaving tomorrow?'

The familiar lump formed in Jess's throat. 'Yup. On the eleven o'clock Eurostar.' Although if things went the way she wanted tonight, then she'd be coming back soon.

'Well, find me on Facebook. Let's keep in touch.'

'Will do.' She wondered if Elodie ever posted pictures of her brother.

'*Au revoir.*'

I'm sure this isn't really goodbye, Jess thought.

From behind the door, she heard an explosion of laughter.

18

AFTER TIDYING THE FLAT, MAKING THE BED, AND GATHERING UP THE few items she hadn't brought to the chateau, Jess returned upstairs, opening Gabriel's door in the middle of one of Johnson's stories.

'And then the waitress says, "That's not a cockroach. *This* is a cockroach!"' Loud laughter ensued and Jess wished that she'd heard the rest of the story, glad that Gabriel was enjoying himself. On the kitchen island, she spotted two open bottles of wine, one already empty.

Uh oh.

She dropped the box containing Pierre the Pig's remains on the counter, threw her other things on the bed in Gabriel's room, and then returned to collect her wine glass. Now, where should she sit? Gabriel and Johnson occupied either side of the olive green sofa, which faced the big bank of windows overlooking the street. It would be too squashed for her to join them, even if she snuggled into Gabriel. Instead, she insinuated herself into an armchair on the other side of the glass coffee table, her back to the windows, and tucked her legs underneath her.

Gabriel hadn't even looked at her since she'd returned. Talk about being a gooseberry.

Jess contemplated the attachment these two must have to each other. To share an experience like a kidnapping bonded them like brothers. There would always be conversations that only the two of them could have.

She shifted in her seat and sipped from her glass, barely listening to them. Instead, she tried to figure out what to say to Gabriel later. How could she convince him to fight for a relationship with her?

A bell sounded.

'Ah, that's dinner,' he announced.

'I'll get it!' Jess jumped up, glad to do something to make herself useful. Neither of them offered to go instead, so engrossed were they in their conversation about a photo story Johnson had shot in Hong Kong. She rode down in the lift and opened the front door to find the waiter from the restaurant standing there, a bulging white take-away bag in his hand with *Severin* written in black marker across its front.

'*Bonne soirée,*' he said as recognition dawned on his weasel face. His smirk said, 'I know what *you've* been up to, young lady.' It made her bridle and feel deeply uncomfortable.

She grabbed the bag and closed the door with a stiff *merci*. The smug look he had given her insinuated that this thing between Gabriel and her was just a dirty shagfest.

'Food's here!' she exclaimed as she walked into the flat. Gabriel and Johnson unfolded themselves from the sofa and moved to the dining table, never once breaking their conversation's flow. She noticed a third bottle of wine had been opened in her absence.

Okay...

Maybe she should pour most of the bottle into her glass and then go empty it into the sink. It's not like they'd notice.

The men seemed in no hurry to set the table, so Jess went to the kitchen to retrieve plates and cutlery for everybody. She claimed the seat next to Gabriel, on his left. She let her leg fall towards him and rubbed her knee against his. His hand reached under the table and briefly squeezed her thigh before departing again—a small acknowledgement, but at least he seemed to know she was still there. Each of them decanted their steak and frites onto their plates.

With a slight slur in his speech, Johnson asked, 'So how did you two meet?' and then shoved a sizeable chunk of steak in his mouth, like he hadn't eaten properly in ages.

It was the first time anybody had asked them this question—a rite of passage in any couple's relationship. In a complete 180 from how the waiter had made her feel, Johnson's question made this feel real, legitimate. Jess smiled and glanced at Gabriel, wondering how he'd tell the story.

'She was drunk and I helped her get back to her flat,' said Gabriel without any embellishment. Jess frowned. That's not how she would have told it. His way made her sound like some wasted tourist that he pulled. What about the fact that she just happened to be staying in his rental flat? What about the spontaneity science fair project? The helicopter? The cloud?

'Wow,' she gulped her wine. 'You make it sound so romantic.'

'Just stating the facts,' he shrugged.

It was like summarising that famous diner orgasm scene in *When Harry Met Sally* as 'woman wants her condiments on the side.'

Gabriel added, 'Jess is heading back to London tomorrow.'

'Oh, bugger,' said Johnson. 'I'm sorry—now I feel like a gatecrasher. I'll leave you two alone after dinner.'

Yes! thought Jess.

'No, don't be ridiculous,' said Gabriel. 'I only get to catch up with you once a year. Jess doesn't mind, do you?' He looked at her with expectant eyes.

There was only one answer. 'No. No, of course not.' A rush of moisture crowded her tear ducts and she blinked rapidly to send it away. Suddenly she wanted to get out of that room as soon as possible. She had gone from having all of Gabriel's attention to having none of it, and she had whiplash from the abrupt change. This man next to her was acting like she was a stranger.

Jess pushed her chair away from the table. 'You know what, I think I'm going to go to bed early. I'm still a bit shaken up from the accident.'

'Accident?' asked Johnson. To his credit, he looked genuinely concerned.

'The car in front of us got taken out by a kid with a death wish,' said Gabriel. Watching his face, Jess saw a brief flicker of pain wash across his features, then he shook his head sharply and it was gone. She had been right. The accident had affected him more than he let on.

'Wow, you two have had an intense evening. I really think I should go.' Johnson started to stand.

'No!' Gabriel practically commanded. And then softer: 'No. I've been saving up a special whiskey for us to toast Fatima this year. You can't go until we've done that.'

Quietly, Jess cleared the plates and then hid in Gabriel's bedroom. She understood that he needed to be alone with Johnson, to share the memories and comfort each other as survivors of the same trauma. Sitting on his bed with her head in her hands, she let the tears she'd been holding back track down her face.

She looked up and her eyes fell on the picture of Fatima. Jess picked it up. She traced the edges of Gabriel's wide smile with her finger and wished that he could regain the *joie de vivre* that he'd had back then. Was that Gabriel gone forever? Or could she help bring him back?

Jess put the picture down and flopped onto the bed. What had she stumbled into? She wanted with all her heart to help Gabriel, but his PTSD was a bigger barrier than she originally thought. She had zero experience dealing with somebody who had been through Gabriel's trials. Maybe she had rose-tinted glasses, but she'd always believed that love conquered all. If she loved him—and she really believed that she did—then they could navigate anything life threw at them.

But love is a two-way street. Was he ever going to be able to love her? She had already been in one relationship where she realised too late that her partner didn't care for her as much as she cared for him. She deserved to be somebody else's moon and stars.

Still, she wasn't going to give up hope yet. They had shared something special at the chateau.

That could be our life, she thought again. *If he'll only let me in.*

Back in the kitchen, she heard the distinct sound of another cork popping.

FOUR HOURS LATER, Gabriel still hadn't come to bed. Jess checked her watch. It was almost one o'clock now.

She couldn't sleep. Disappointment, heartsickness and sadness tumbled through her, making it impossible to pass out. And she was thirsty.

Finding a robe on the back of his bathroom door, she put it on and padded out on bare feet towards the kitchen. She'd just slip in without disturbing them, using the hallway entrance to get to the glasses.

The mood in the room was a lot less raucous than earlier. She peeked around the corner of the cupboards and saw they were slumped on the sofa again. From her vantage point, all she saw were the crowns of their heads, resting on the back cushions. On the coffee table beyond, she noticed a whiskey bottle had joined the wine bottles.

Johnson was talking in a low, slurred voice about how he went back into therapy after they last saw each other. It seemed to be working: he had better control of his emotions lately, the nightmares had stopped, and he'd made some big strides in his personal life.

Jess definitely shouldn't be listening to this. She retrieved a glass from the cupboard as quietly as possible, trying to stay out of sight even though they were facing away from her. She'd fill it up in the bathroom.

Just when she was about to sneak back, she heard Johnson say, 'What about you, man? What's up with this woman? Is it serious?'

She assumed that 'this woman' was her. She held her breath, knowing she shouldn't be there, but giving in to her base desire to hear his reply.

'Jess?' Gabriel said, his deep voice sounding tired as he huffed a humourless laugh. 'It's nothing. Just a holiday fling. You know me—I'll die alone.'

'That's too bad, mate. She seems nice.'

Pressing her lips together, Jess fought the tears that flooded her eyes again, and completely failed. If she didn't get back to the bedroom soon, they might hear her sob. She ran on tiptoes and shut the door silently behind her. Falling onto his bed, she buried her face in a pillow and let the tears flow freely.

What a complete and utter idiot she'd been.

Of course, it was just a fling. Deep down she knew that. Somehow her heart had tricked her into thinking it was more. *Stupid, stupid woman.*

She should have known better. It would have been too neat—breaking up with one man and jumping straight into a relationship with another. Life didn't work like that and it probably wasn't healthy. *What are you doing?* she thought. She'd just traded in her own problems for somebody else's. She turned on her side and hugged her knees to her chest, her eyes falling on the picture of Fatima again.

What was Jess even doing here? She didn't belong in Gabriel's room. She was an interloper here. Again. For a few days, he had opened the door and let her in, but now it was time to leave with her head held high. No scenes. She'd just go and let this whole experience become a memory. She'd return to London and get on with rebuilding her life, alone. That would be the best thing for her: to spend some time on her own.

Gulping hard, she pushed herself off the bed and changed out of her camisole into jeans, a shirt, and the pink hoodie she'd bought for the helicopter ride. She packed the rest of her things into her suitcase, even making room for the witchy cookie jar. It felt like a symbol of something...witches were strong women who chose to live on their own terms, alone if necessary. Or perhaps it was just a reminder to protect her heart better in the future. Either way, she wanted to keep it.

She opened the door to the bedroom and listened. The talking had stopped and now she just heard two sets of snores coming from the living room. Great. She would slip past, crash in the rental flat, and leave early in the morning for the train station. From the razor-like snorts she knew weren't Gabriel's, it sounded like Johnson would be sleeping on the couch after all.

Taking a step, she stopped herself. She should leave a note. She realised she still didn't have his phone number, so she couldn't just send him a goodbye text. Yes, a note. Gabriel deserved that. Even though things didn't end how she would have liked, they had shared something...well, in her mind, at least.

Jess ripped a page out of the notepad she always carried in her sack of a handbag and dug out a pen. What should she say? Nothing too long. Just something from the heart. She scribbled her message onto the paper and left it next to the picture of Fatima.

Then she silently left the apartment.

19

GABRIEL WOKE UP ON HIS SOFA WITH A WEIGHT ACROSS HIS LEGS. HE blinked into the morning light streaming through the windows. The empty wine bottles on the coffee table sparkled in the sun's rays, momentarily blinding him.

Shielding his eyes, he looked down towards his lap at two blistered feet. He followed the legs up to the face to find Johnson passed out, a line of drool running out of the corner of his mouth.

Gabriel sat up and cringed. His head throbbed with pain. Damn Johnson. Whenever he came around, Gabriel ended up drinking like a British heathen. Unfortunately, that seemed to be the only way they'd come up with between them to handle the weight of their shared memories.

Happy birthday, Fatima, he thought.

You forgetting something, you inconsiderate douchebag? her voice replied.

He stilled for a moment and listened. Aside from Johnson's ragged snores, the apartment was totally quiet.

Fuck.

Where was Jess?

Panicking, he pushed Johnson's feet off his lap and stood, needing a moment to get his balance. His stump itched from being in the silicon sock for too long. Usually, he took it off to sleep after washing his stump thoroughly, but last night he'd passed out without doing his ablutions. Johnson and he really needed to stop this destructive routine they had going. Gabriel was getting too old for this shit.

Still dizzy, he stumbled to his bedroom to find it empty. Her bag was gone. He checked his watch. It said 10AM, but he didn't know what time her train was leaving from the station. Thinking they'd have last night, they'd never discussed it.

His eye caught on the piece of paper next to Fatima's picture. With a sinking feeling, he limped over and read it.

> Dear Gabriel,
> Thank you for taking care of me this week. I'll never forget it. Please be kind to yourself and remember to smile. Hoping you find happiness one day. You deserve it.
> Jess x

The words sliced like daggers. What had he done?

Yesterday, after the accident, his brain broke. That was the only way he could think to describe it. Between the intrusive thoughts about how Jess could have died swirling in his head, mixed with the appearance of Johnson and all the memories and feelings he brought with him, Gabriel's brain short-circuited. It was like the real Gabriel was trapped in a glass cage inside and was screaming to get out, but the Gabriel-in-Charge ignored it. He pushed it away, like he'd ignored and pushed Jess away last night. He just couldn't handle the world he'd carefully built with her over the past few days colliding with the one he shared with Fatima and Johnson.

He read the note again.

A feeling swelled in his chest. One part nausea, one part fear, but most parts regret. Now that she'd gone, he knew he wasn't ready to say goodbye yet. The last few days had reminded him of the person he used to be, but better. He liked it. Jess was the person who helped to free the Gabriel in the cage.

And he'd let her leave without saying goodbye.

Somewhere in the apartment, he heard the sounds of retching. Johnson must be up.

No matter. Gabriel had to find Jess. Quickly, he took off his prosthesis, wiped out the socket, cleaned his stump, found a new sock, and put it back on again. He wouldn't be able to walk properly unless he tended to it, and not doing it would just hold him back. It took him less than two minutes. Just as fast, he changed his clothes, took two headache pills and, as an afterthought, downed some antacids to manage the results of his hangover. Brushing his teeth, he noticed that she'd left her toothbrush behind and he was struck with the urge to cuddle it.

Shaking his head, he located his phone on the kitchen island and dialled his sister.

'*Allo?*' she answered.

'Hey, do you know what time Jess's train is taking off today?' he said, desperation colouring his voice.

She scoffed, 'Nice to hear from you, too.'

'Elodie!'

With an exasperating know-it-all tone, she said, 'As a matter of fact, I do.'

He waited. 'Okay.' Dead air. 'Are you going to tell me?'

'*Bof.*' She seemed in no hurry. This was no time for games. Her attitude made him want to scream, in a way only little sisters could provoke. 'First spill the beans. What happened? Did you and Johnson get blazing drunk?'

'Yes.'

'And did you pass out?'

'Yes.'

'And did Jess decide she didn't need your bullshit and leave your ass?'

He gulped, his heart crumpling like a tin can. The sickness in his stomach had nothing to do with his hangover. 'Yes.'

'You're a complete dickhead. You know that?'

Ha. She's right. For the first time, he realised the voice in his head sounded like both Fatima and his sister. They were ganging up on him. 'C'mon! Just fucking tell me.' His patience wore thin.

'Eleven o'clock. You'll never make it.' She sounded both angry and disappointed in him.

'Watch me.' He hung up the phone.

It was a quarter past ten now. It would take him roughly twenty minutes to get to the Gare du Nord. He'd worry about what happened next when he arrived.

Johnson emerged from the guest bathroom, wiping a towel over his face.

'I'm never drinking again,' he moaned. 'You're a bad influence.'

Gabriel rolled his eyes. They were both as bad as each other. 'I'm heading out. Make yourself at home.'

'Where are you going?'

Already halfway out the door, Gabriel called out, 'To stop Jess from leaving!' The door clicked closed. He pushed the button and waited for the lift.

He wasn't a praying man. He'd seen too much death and destruction and evil in the world to believe in any benevolent higher power. But he prayed now. *God, please let me get there on time. Don't let her leave.*

JESS SAT in a coffee shop at the Gare du Nord, letting her cappuccino grow cold. Through the window, she stared at the bustle of people either rushing into the station to catch their trains or rushing out to catch a taxi. Determined pigeons navigated the assault course of legs, searching for crumbs. Jess hardly saw any of it.

Krish had bought them first-class tickets for the Eurostar, which meant she didn't have to head through security until twenty minutes before departure. It was currently 10:30. People in the cafe existed around her, chatting, checking their phones, and working on laptops. Jess was there among them, but absent at the same time. She knew she should go, but just couldn't seem to get out of her seat, like she was waiting for something. Or someone. She sighed. With the amount of alcohol Gabriel and Johnson drank last night, they'd probably be passed out all morning. She remembered that he had an important meeting with his agent this afternoon and hoped he wouldn't miss it.

It's not your problem anymore, Jess.

The words *'it's nothing'* rang in her ears. Did he really mean that? Or was he just trying to protect himself from admitting he had feelings for her? Either way, she hated that they hadn't said goodbye properly. Even though she'd left a note, it felt like she still needed closure.

Funny that she'd never put his mobile number in her phone. If she had, then she'd probably have texted him by now, which made her glad that she didn't have it. He had hers. He could call her when he was ready. If he was ever ready. It felt old school, almost romantic that she didn't have it.

'We'll always have Paris,' she thought, remembering the scene in *Casablanca* where Rick bids farewell to Ilsa at the airport. No mobile

phones there. Just the conviction of their memories. That's what she'd take away with her.

A rogue tear slipped down her cheek.

Jess hadn't slept a wink last night—hoping that Gabriel might come to find her, worrying that Johnson might barge into the flat (even though she'd reinforced the lock from the inside). When her alarm went off at 8AM, it took all her willpower not to go upstairs and kiss him one more time. But the words *'It's nothing'* kept her away, plus he would probably be in no fit state for an emotional farewell. She'd rather leave with her memories of him intact, just like Rick and Ilsa.

Last night had been tough. She saw yet another side of Gabriel, which scared her slightly. Between the accident, Johnson's arrival, and her leaving, it was a perfect storm. Too much for him to handle. No wonder he spent so much time doing calm things: tending his plants and his Japanese pottery and listening to classical music.

The memory of her introduction to Beethoven momentarily overwhelmed her and she squeezed her thighs together to prolong the sensations. It passed. Just like these feelings would pass. As she realised on the helicopter ride, life went on. She'd survive.

Unlike her past relationships, for once she was the one doing the leaving, but it didn't feel as empowering as she'd imagined it would. It felt like shit. This wasn't how she wanted to end things, but what choice did she have? Even with her rose-tinted glasses on, the message had been clear: Gabriel was not ready for a relationship. Regardless of whether he was the right guy, it wasn't the right time.

It made her realise something about herself, too: she wasn't ready either. Only a week had passed since Krish broke up with her. Even though she believed her feelings for Gabriel were genuine, part of her was still mourning for the relationship that had just ended. It wouldn't be fair to either her or Gabriel to rush into anything right now. She needed to be alone for a while and learn to trust her instincts again. Eventually, she'd heal and be ready to move forward —if not with Gabriel, with somebody else.

Her heart clenched at the idea, making her breath catch.

She looked at the time on her watch. 10:35. With a last longing look through the window, she gathered her things and made her way to the Eurostar terminal.

GABRIEL TRIED AGAIN with the jobsworth manning the ticket scanners.

'Please, I have to find somebody before she leaves for London. Can I go through for a couple of minutes?' He smiled his friendliest smile—not a natural facial expression for him.

The short man twiddled one end of his handlebar moustache and said, 'Do you have a ticket?'

'No.'

With exaggerated regret on his unimpressed face, he tsked and said, 'No un-ticketed passengers beyond this point.'

Gabriel put one hand on his waist and one hand on his pounding forehead. 'You said that already.'

'Well, you obviously didn't hear me the first time.' The man checked someone else's ticket and answered her question before helping her pass through the booths.

Gabriel decided to open up to this stranger in one last attempt to melt his cold, cold heart. 'Please…haven't you ever regretted letting someone go? If she gets on that train, I'll regret it for the rest of my life.'

The man's gaze turned soft, like he was remembering the One That Got Away. 'Yes…her name was Beatrice. And she made the best *boeuf bourguignon* north of Burgundy…'

'So you'll let me through?'

The ticket agent actually laughed. 'No. You people watch too many movies.'

Gabriel threw up his hands and swore. What was he going to do? He fought the temptation to grab the ends of the man's moustache and tug.

Another ticket agent—tall and lanky this time—joined the first one. 'Is there a problem here?' he sing-songed with the distinct accent of somebody from Marseille.

'Yes!' said Gabriel, hoping he might have a better chance with this one. Marseillais were known for being friendlier than Parisians. 'I need to go through. There's a girl—'

'Ah, there's always a girl,' he agreed in his slow drawl and nodded at Moustache Man, who also nodded.

'—And I need to catch her before she gets on the train.'

To his colleague, the second ticket agent said, 'You know, I once heard a story about a ticket officer who let a man through because he declared that he needed to proclaim his undying love to a passenger.'

'And?'

'And it turned out that he was her stalker, not her boyfriend. By all accounts, it got veeee-ry messy.'

Gabriel pasted on his best smile again. 'Do I look like a stalker?'

The man flicked his eyes up and down Gabriel's tall, muscular frame and shrugged. 'You could be the reincarnation of Joseph Vacher for all I know. Just in case, the answer is no.'

'Gabriel?'

He whipped around to find Jess standing behind him. The dark circles under her eyes cut him straight to the bone. She'd obviously had a bad night's sleep, thanks to him. She wore her *'Paris je t'aime'* sweatshirt, which reminded him of their trip in the helicopter. For a moment, he froze, unsure what to say.

'Oh, she's very pretty,' said agent number one.

'Yes, I agree. Very pretty,' agreed number two.

Oblivious to the commentary of the French ticket agents, Jess parked her bag next to her and crossed her arms. 'What are you doing here?'

The moustachioed ticket man said in Poirot-style English, 'Iz he a stalker, madam? Should we call ze police?'

Her brow drew down in confusion. 'Um, no. That's okay.'

Gabriel shook his head to clear his shock at finding her. He had a lot to say and not a lot of time to say it. 'Jess, I'm sorry about last night. I know—it's not an excuse, but I got overwhelmed.'

'It's okay, Gabriel. I understand. You don't owe me an explanation.' She shrugged one shoulder. 'It was just a fling, right?'

'Don't say that. You know that's not true.'

'Isn't it? That's what you said to Johnson last night.'

He winced and cursed himself. 'I was in a bad place. I'm sorry. I didn't mean it.'

She raised her gaze to his, and he saw the bright sheen of unshed tears. He hated that he did this to her. He felt like the world's biggest asshole. 'Listen, Gabriel, I'm grateful for everything you've done for me. Truly. You've opened my eyes—in many ways.' She blushed. 'And you really helped me through some difficult days. But you and I both knew what this was: two people, who needed each other for a short time. Let's just leave it at that.'

He couldn't believe she was saying this. He had been sure that she felt the same sense of...of *rightness* between them. What happened to *I think I'm falling in love with you?* He had royally fucked things up. 'I don't want you to go.'

She swallowed and closed her eyes like she was gathering strength for what she had to say next. His stomach sank. 'Maybe we could have had something, but neither one of us is ready. I just broke up with Krish and you...you have work to do. I saw that last night.'

With an exasperated sigh, he said, 'Seeing Johnson is always going to bring up bad memories—'

'Bad memories? Gabriel, you ignored me and made me feel like I didn't mean anything to you.'

'I know, and I'm sorry. I couldn't control it…'

'You need help, Gabriel. Help that I'm not qualified to give you.'

He reached for her and she pulled back her hand. The easy camaraderie they'd shared at the chateau had disintegrated. He didn't have her permission to touch her anymore. 'I really messed up, didn't I?'

'Well, yes. But like I said, I'm not ready either.' She smiled sadly.

Unsure what else to do with them, he shoved his hands in his jean pockets. 'So this is goodbye?'

'Yes, I think so.'

Inside he panicked that their reunion was playing out like this. His whole being cried out for her, but she was pushing him away. If she didn't want him, then she didn't want him. Maybe he was just too big of a mess for a relationship. That's why he'd avoided them for eight years, after all. He couldn't exactly disagree with her. But he couldn't let her go without touching her one more time.

'Can I say goodbye to you properly?'

Jess bit her lip, and her pupils dilated with want. At least he knew she still felt the attraction between them. 'I think that would be acceptable.' She stepped towards him and slid her hands behind his neck. Electricity followed the trail of her fingers. Gabriel gripped her waist, holding her tight.

Their eyes locked, and he saw a whole world of regret in their blue depths. He wondered what she saw in his. In a flash their lips came together, their tongues instantly tangling, seeking out the other. Heat rushed through him, and his heart cried out like it had all the other times he'd kissed her. Only now, he was more receptive to the message. It said: *this one is special.*

He wanted their kiss to go on forever. The idea of her walking away from him made his chest hurt like he'd been punched.

Too soon, the last boarding call for her train sounded over the loudspeaker, and she broke contact. 'I have to go.'

Gabriel pressed his forehead against hers. 'I know,' he whispered.

'Look me up if you ever visit London,' she said as she stepped away. He noticed the skin of her fingers turning white where she clasped the suitcase handle tightly and understood that this wasn't easy for her either.

'Bye, Gabriel.'

'*Au revoir*, Jess.'

And with that, she scanned her ticket and walked through the barriers. Each step she took away from him felt like a string being pulled tauter and tauter, like a piece of him was leaving.

He heard a sniffle to his left. 'Go after her, *espèce d'idiot*!' cried the moustachioed ticket man, using his key card to open the gate. 'Go tell her that you love her!'

Love? Was that what this was? If yes, no wonder he'd avoided it all his life. He thought he'd already run the gamut of heartache and regret, but this sorrow in his chest was a completely new type of pain. With Fatima's death, the grief had been scissor-sharp. As he watched Jess walk away, this feeling was more like a balloon inflating beneath his ribs, stealing all his air.

But she was right. He fucked up. He *was* fucked up. He couldn't be the man she needed, his performance last night proved that. They'd only been together for less than a week and he had already failed.

Perhaps the best way to prove his love was to let her go.

20

JESS PUSHED OPEN THE DOOR OF HER FLAT AND TOOK A DEEP BREATH before crossing the threshold.

Home sweet home, she thought as she surveyed the living room/kitchen area. The Juliette balcony offered views across the rooftops of London, along with a flat grey sky. It mirrored her mood.

She massaged her puffy eyes. They'd had a workout on the train journey, rubbed raw from the dozens of tissues she'd used to wipe her tears.

Walking away from Gabriel was the hardest thing she'd ever done. His face when she said it was just a fling made her want to immediately retract it and tell him that she did love him.

But what would be the point? Even though it broke her heart, she knew she'd made the right choice. He had so many issues to sort out, and she would have happily stood by his side while he worked on them, but he'd made it pretty clear from his actions that he wasn't ready for that. The moment things got tough, he'd locked her out.

Truly, she wanted him to get better and find happiness, even if it wasn't with her. The thought made her chest tighten painfully and her shoulders droop.

'Welcome to your new home,' she said to the witchy cookie jar as she took it out of her bag and set it on the shelf with her other cookie jars. Its closest neighbour was a pink elephant with a blue hat. She had a feeling they'd get on just fine.

So...what should she do next? How did single people normally occupy their time? She'd had a significant other for years. Entertainment at the touch of a button. If Krish and she were still together, they might have gone for a run, or she might have gone up to his flat, or cooked them dinner. But they weren't together. Her time was 100% hers, and she didn't know what to do with it.

Her eyes fell on the Cornish painting that Krish bought for her on their first holiday together. That could go. A casual sweep of the room with her eyes identified at least ten more things that she'd happily part with. Even though she felt exhausted from the travel and lack of sleep, the desire to de-Krish her flat overcame her, filling her with much-needed adrenaline.

She took off her sweatshirt and got to work.

COMING out about her and Krish was easier than she thought. She phoned her closest friends to tell them first. Everyone was shocked but supportive, offering to organise girly nights and inviting her to parties. Ankita, Krish's sister, made dinner plans with Jess, then had to cancel them due to the early arrival of her baby. When she couldn't put it off any longer, Jess changed her relationship status on Facebook to single. She had an instant deluge of messages, but then they died down quickly. Turns out, people didn't really care. Who knew?

She didn't tell anyone about Gabriel. He was her secret.

THE SCHOOL YEAR started much the same as any other school year: with a lot of kids who had been free range all summer and now needed to relearn the rules of the classroom. Within a week, one little girl had vomited on Jess's shoes, two little boys stuck building bricks up their noses, and one mother scheduled a meeting with Jess to discuss her plan for accelerating her five-year-old's reading level.

It kept her busy, and Jess enjoyed it. Not a day went by that her kids didn't make her laugh and fill her with hope for the future. When it was her birthday, they made her a card and signed it, each one of their messy stick-figure signatures feeling like an accomplishment to Jess.

It was her nights that tortured her.

At night, she had time to think. At night, she remembered what it felt like to make love with Gabriel, the touch of his hand, the fit of his body against hers, the unbelievable orgasms that started deep within and radiated out. Strangely, she didn't think about sex with Krish at all. It hadn't been bad between them, but it hadn't been explosive either. The things she'd done with Gabriel were the ones that plagued her.

Eventually, the memory of being with him would pass. In the meantime, she bought her first vibrator.

The delivery driver left the package with a neighbour, the little old lady in number ten. Jess received the notification when she was at school and all day, she worried that her neighbour would know what was in the box, even though the website promised that there was nothing on the outside that indicated what was inside. When Jess returned home, she rushed straight to number ten to collect her illicit delivery, sure that her bright red face revealed the story that the unmarked packaging did not.

Back in her flat, she unwrapped the toy: a big pink number with a rabbit and three vibration settings. She charged it up straight away and then counted the hours until bedtime.

It did not disappoint. Not the same as being with Gabriel in the flesh—the orgasms were too fast and very surface, far from the full body experience she'd enjoyed with him. But they were enough to pleasure her and give her imagination plenty of ammunition.

But she really missed Gabriel.

THE IDEA for the skydive came to her while she was looking through Elodie's Facebook page. Yes, Jess had succumbed. In fact, she'd friended Elodie while traveling on the Eurostar.

The trigger that sparked the idea was a picture of Gabriel. He'd mentioned that he was running a 10k for charity, and there he was, wearing his running blade and looking just as hot as Jess remembered him. The photo wasn't posed. In fact, Jess doubted that Gabriel even knew his sister had taken it. He was shirtless—Jess spent quite some time zooming in on his chest and studying the line of hair that disappeared behind the elastic of his shorts—but he was looking away, his customary frown pulling down the corners of his lips. Jess ached to take him in her arms and make him smile again.

Recently, Jess listened to a podcast about choosing a power word. She'd been consuming a lot of podcasts since she returned, mostly to do with self-improvement—although she also loved the BBC Comedy shows. Anyway, this podcast said that she should choose a power word to help her set her intentions on how she wanted to live for the next twelve months, and the word Jess chose was *challenge*. She wanted to push herself out of her comfort zone and seeing the picture of Gabriel made her want to raise money for charity.

Running a marathon would be a definite activity on her list, but what else could she do? She remembered that one of her work colleagues had skydived the previous spring, raving about it afterwards. At the time, Jess never would have considered something like that, but now she didn't feel like that Jess anymore. Now she wanted to live large, worry less.

And part of her hoped she could recapture some of that feeling she'd had in the helicopter with Gabriel, when she'd touched a cloud and experienced that transcendent sense of connection.

It didn't take long to set up. All she had to do was choose a company with which to entrust her life, book the dive, find the charity she wanted to help, and create a fundraising page. She chose a date during half-term in October for the jump. Within an hour, it was done and dusted. No backing out now.

She splashed it across her socials and people started donating right away. Her dad started it off with £50. Within a week, she'd made her target, so she upped it again.

Next step: she just had to wait eight weeks and try not to think about the fact that she was *jumping out of a fucking plane.*

21

'*Bonjour!*' Gabriel heard Elodie call as she entered his apartment. Uninvited. Again.

'Go away!' he replied. His stump spasmed, and he bit his tongue, refusing to give Elodie the satisfaction of hearing him cry out.

His phantom limb pains had returned with a vengeance. Every 30 seconds or so, lightning flared underneath his skin. In the past when they bothered him, they usually lasted for five or six hours, max, eventually fading by themselves. This round had been going strong for three days already. And he hadn't slept since they began.

Zombies had more vitality than he did right now. And it didn't help that Elodie kept popping in to check on him.

Speaking of the devil, she stood in his doorway now, arms crossed and glaring at him. 'I take it they're still going.'

Gabriel winced as another pain flashed through his stump.

'It's never gone on this long before. Why do you think it's happening now?' She tilted her head at him with her eyebrows raised like she already knew the answer. Typical teacher move.

He knew the answer, too, but didn't want to acknowledge it. Any amateur psychologist could figure out the problem: his brain was trying to communicate with a part of him that was no longer there.

Jess.

She'd been gone for two weeks and he'd been miserable since she left. Food tasted bland; the sun failed to warm him; hearing laughter made him frown. If he didn't watch out, he'd turn into an actual hermit, and the children in the neighbourhood would start making up stories about him. '*There goes the* Le Bossu de Montmartre. *Watch out for him. At night he transforms into a rat and drinks the tears of virgins*' or something like that.

Another pain crackled under his scars.

'Argh!'

The angry look in Elodie's eyes was replaced by pity. He hated being pitied. 'Gabriel, you can't go on like this. You need to get some help. I'm sure if you called Dr Reynaud he would fit you into his schedule.'

Gabriel turned his head away and glared at the wall. He remembered his last session with Dr Reynaud two years ago, where the good doctor suggested that Gabriel should try opening himself up to relationships. Gabriel had scoffed at the idea, told the doctor that he thought he was full of shit, and left halfway through the session. 'What are you so scared of?' the doctor had called after him.

This. Exactly this. Uncontrollable pain. Worrying about another person above all others. Being vulnerable. All of this scared the crap out of him and now that he was living it, he knew why.

Love sucks.

'Have you tried to contact her at all?' Elodie asked, making herself comfortable next to him on the bed.

Gabriel pulled a face that said *don't be ridiculous*. 'No, of course not. She made her feelings clear. It was just sex.'

'Oh yeah? How do you explain this?' She pulled out her phone and opened up Facebook.

It showed a stock picture of someone jumping out of a plane. 'What am I looking at?' he asked.

'This, you dummy!' She pointed to a line of copy under the picture: *Can you help Jess raise money for...*

The words faded out.

'So?'

Elodie stabbed the screen with her finger and another screen popped up. 'So?! She's jumping out of a plane to raise money for children who need prostheses. Do you think she would have done that before meeting you?'

He shrugged and gritted his teeth as another pain shot through him. 'Probably. She's a very kind person.'

Contrary to his calm demeanour, his heart thumped faster. Jess was jumping out of a plane. Without him there. Apparently her spontaneity science fair project lived on. That was good. But also, scary. What if she hurt herself? He would do some research into the company, make sure they were a professional outfit.

Elodie grunted with exasperation and hit him on his leg.

'Ow!'

'That's not what I mean! I mean the fact that she chose to raise money for a charity that just happens to support people like you. But smaller and cuter and probably smarter.'

'What of it?' Dating a shrink had obviously turned his sister into a licensed psychologist.

'You really don't know anything about women, do you.' It wasn't a question.

'Elodie, stop. I'm no good for her. I couldn't even go one week without fucking things up.'

In a rare display of physical affection, Elodie reached out and touched him on the cheek. 'Gabriel, what are you scared of?'

The question echoed what his psychiatrist had asked him. He huffed bitterly and pushed her hand away. 'Me? I'm scared of everything. I'm scared of losing everybody I love. Which includes you, if you'd believe it. I'm scared of feeling too much. Living too little. Being vulnerable. I'm scared that I'll never feel again like I did with Jess at the chateau.'

She pursed her lips, and her concerned gaze bore into him. 'Do you love her?'

Another pain. After it passed he said, 'It doesn't matter if I love her.'

Grabbing his shoulders, she asked again, 'Do. You. Love. Her?'

Did he love Jess?

Well, he missed her smile. He missed the way she bit her lip after making a joke, as though waiting to see if it landed properly. He missed her enthusiasm for life. He missed her bravery. He missed the way she made him feel invincible. He missed the way he fit inside her like she'd been made for him. He missed the feeling of security he had when she was around. He missed seeing the expression of wonder on her face when she experienced something new. He missed holding her in his arms. Did he love her?

'Yes,' he whispered, dropping his head into his hands.

'Then that solves everything,' Elodie said.

LATER THAT DAY, Gabriel called Dr Reynaud. The good doctor gave him an appointment for that evening.

The power of the mind both terrified and awed Gabriel. As soon as he'd made the decision to get help, to try to become a man that was worthy of Jess, his pain stopped. Just like that.

Thank fuck you're getting help. I'm tired of being your excuse, said Fatima's voice in his head. He huffed a laugh.

You're a pain in my ass, he thought.

Always. He pictured her cheeky wink.

189

He had a feeling he wouldn't be hearing from her any time soon.

When he'd returned to the apartment after seeing Jess at the station, Johnson was still there, waiting for him. Johnson sat him down for a heart-to-heart. It was the first time that they didn't hide their feelings in reminiscences and alcohol. His old friend confessed that one of the reasons he wanted to see Gabriel was to invite him to his wedding. He'd met a woman while he was based in Singapore last year and they fell in love. She was the one who had pushed Johnson to seek help again and to stick with it, rather than giving up after a few months like previous times. Her name was Yvonne and her family was rich as fuck and apparently she had the hottest arse in the East (she was a fitness influencer on Instagram). But also a really amazing person. Gabriel was happy for his friend.

Unexpectedly, Johnson had then taken Gabriel by the shoulders and said, 'You know, you need to move past what happened, G. You have to forgive yourself. You couldn't have done anything to stop Fatima's death. It was nobody's fault.'

Although Gabriel had heard those same words on many occasions from many people, it was the first time he actually listened.

It may have taken two more weeks and a kick up the bum from his sister, but Gabriel finally felt ready to heal.

He just hoped he could make some progress before it was too late for him and Jess.

22

Today was the big day and Jess wanted to vomit.

Her inner scaredy cat, which she tried to listen to less these days, hoped to receive a cancellation message from the skydive company, but nope. The day dawned blue and clear. No October weather warnings in sight. In fact, it was unseasonably warm.

Last night, she'd stayed at her parents' house to make driving to the drop zone easier. Over breakfast, she was so nervous that she spilt her tea all over her parents' floral waxed tablecloth that they'd had since she was born. As she wiped it up, she said to her dad, 'Remind me again why I decided it would be a good idea to do this?'

Her dad shook his head and pursed his lips dramatically. 'No idea, pumpkin. You wouldn't catch me dead jumping out of a plane.'

She rolled her eyes. Not the assurance she wanted. 'Thanks, daddy.'

'Just make sure they give you one of those parachutes that opens.' He patted her on the hand and returned his attention to the newspaper.

The person she really wanted to talk to about this hadn't been in touch with her since she'd left Paris. Not for the first time, she wondered what Gabriel would say to her if he saw her now. Something about her spontaneity science fair project paying off. Heck, he'd probably want to do it with her.

Jess thought about her week in Paris and Gabriel every day. From her heart to her lady parts, so many areas of her ached whenever she remembered their brief escape to the chateau. She spent more time than she should have done examining Elodie's Facebook page, which suddenly seemed to be a font of Gabriel porn—well, not porn, but just a lot of pictures. It did not pass Jess by that Elodie's feed *before* Jess went to Paris had been mostly devoid of her brother, but *after* seemed to be a veritable shrine to him. Jess liked to think it was for her benefit, and she appreciated it (she liked every photo).

She'd even started listening to classical music. The other day, in the middle of a random Spotify playlist, a classical piano version of 'Thunderstruck' mixed with the third movement of Beethoven's 'Moonlight Sonata' came on. Her mouth fell open, and she double-checked the song info to make sure she wasn't going crazy. In the end, she'd played it ten times and, afterwards, she went to bed to sort herself out with her pink friend because the memories it evoked turned her on so intensely.

When she went to sleep at night, it wasn't the life she almost had with Krish that she dreamed about, but the one she could have had with Gabriel. She'd heard through the Ankita Grapevine that Krish and Francesca were engaged. Apparently, he popped the question while they were travelling in Rajasthan—a last-minute trip they took before Francesca went into hospital for an operation (Ankita didn't supply all the details, so Jess didn't know what the operation was for). Jess expected to feel a kernel of jealousy at the news...but she didn't. Even the speed at which Krish had proposed didn't bother her. She wished them all the best. Truly. Her heart had moved on, even if the man it settled on wasn't physically in her life anymore.

Even now, thinking about Gabriel was a full-body experience for her. She missed him. Not just his touch, but him. His dry sense of humour, his sensitivity, the way he challenged her and made her take risks. To feel closer to him, she started learning French on a language app. Her skills were slowly improving, and she had aced giving directions and discussing items on a menu—although in one section, it turned a bit macabre and asked her to translate 'Where shall we hide the bodies?' and taught her to describe where various family members in La Rochelle kept their shovels.

Perhaps she'd take another trip to Paris in the summer holidays, drop into Gabriel's gallery and say *Bonjour*, show off her linguistic talents—and she wasn't necessarily talking about her French.

Jess exhaled as she drove into the skydive company's car park and found a free space.

When she left Paris, she told him to look her up if he ever came to London. Would he take her up on that? For the first few weeks, every time her phone rang or a message beeped, a surge of hope filled her. Maybe it was Gabriel! But it never was.

At some point she'd need to move on. One of her work colleagues kept trying to set Jess up with her brother, a hedge fund manager in the City, but Jess didn't feel ready. After Krish and then Gabriel, her heart had been shredded enough. Every week, her friend sent a new picture of her brother with a question mark. He had a fine square jaw and filled out a suit like a Hugo Boss model, but whenever Jess thought about saying yes, her heart said no.

And then there were Elodie's Facebook pictures. Lately, Gabriel was smiling in them. For some undefinable reason, that gave Jess hope, too.

Right now, though, she had other things to worry about—like the fact that she was about to jump out of a plane.

She had chosen this company because it promised views of Stonehenge from the air as she plummeted to the ground. If she was going to perish, at least she'd perish near one of her country's most popular historical attractions.

The correspondence repeated many times that she couldn't be late, as they had to perform an induction and training before the jump and had multiple full flights scheduled throughout the day. Through her windshield, she spied the plane resting on the airfield nearby. To her, it looked a little flimsy. A puddle jumper. Her breathing sped up, and her palms turned sweaty. Gripping the steering wheel, she observed other people getting out of their cars and heading to the self-check-in area, and vaguely thought she should probably join them. She blinked hard.

Come on, Jess, you can do this.

The deep voice in her head spoke with an American accent.

She checked her watch and saw that she had to report to reception in minutes for check-in, so she counted to three and bolted out of the car, taking only a small bag containing her phone and water bottle. She crossed the grass to join the queue of other jumpers at the reception tent. In front of her stood a father and son, who couldn't be more than sixteen years old. *If he can jump, I can jump*, she thought. *Remember, you're doing it for the children.*

When choosing a charity, she'd decided to raise money for one that helped child amputees in poorer countries to get the prostheses they needed, but couldn't afford. Her original goal was quickly exceeded when an anonymous donor gave generously. She noticed that the amount was exactly how much she'd paid to rent the flat in Paris.

At last count, she had raised almost £2,000 and hopefully more would come in today as she did the deed.

Too soon, she was sitting in a room watching a video about what to expect from the day. She glanced at the faces of the other thirty or so fellow crazy people as an enthusiastic Aussie assured them they'd have the time of their lives. Jess would just have to take his word for it. Right now, her heart was thumping and her foot, tapping. Next, the instructor spent fifteen minutes getting them kitted up in their jumpsuits and teaching them the body positions for free fall and landing. 'Arms out, legs up,' Jess repeated under her breath like a mantra as she hung from the parachute simulator.

For some ridiculous reason, she had chosen the higher jump at 15,000 feet when she signed up, which would give her a full minute of free fall. She cursed the past version of herself that ticked that box. She'd also bought the package that included a photographer just so she had some evidence of this insanity to show her donors.

The waiting was the worst part. After their training, they had to sit in a holding room until their slot came up. Jess stared at the company's logo, printed in bright purple on the opposite wall, and tried to stop her teeth from chattering. The clear, windless weather meant that it was running smoothly. To distract herself, Jess decided to make small talk with her other jumpers, the oldest of whom was seventy years old. He reassured her that this was his fifth jump, and she'd love it.

She calmed down after that.

But then her anxiety shot right up again as they climbed into the plane. It seemed way too small to hold as many people as it did; she counted eleven, not including the pilot. The atmosphere was jolly. The other jumpers whooped and high-fived, but Jess just wanted to concentrate on not hyperventilating.

The jumpers snuggled together on the floor, reminding Jess of that game she played with her kids where they all had to sit between each other's legs in a line and pretend to be on Toad's Wild Ride. Like babies in a front-loaded papoose, each of her fellow jumpers was attached to a tandem instructor. Jess found herself harnessed to a stocky Norwegian adrenaline junkie named Kjell. He introduced her to her photographer. She missed his name in the roar of the plane's engines, but he had a tinted visor like the Stig from *Top Gear* and he appeared ready for business with the cameras attached to his helmet. At least she'd receive high-quality memorabilia of her screaming her head off. He nodded and saluted at her.

'Arms out, legs up,' she mumbled under her breath. She sat closest to the slatted door, through which she could see the tarmac rushing past outside. The rattling and the roaring made it hard to concentrate. She closed her eyes to try and block it all out.

She wished Gabriel were here. She remembered how safe she'd felt in his presence on the helicopter. In her head, she imagined it wasn't England, but Paris below her. Opening her eyes, she peered through the open slats of the door to search for a cloud in the blue sky. There, in the distance, just like she remembered them. *Toy Story* clouds. Only one or two, but their presence helped her calm her racing heart and pretend that Gabriel was with her. She breathed in, almost believing that she smelled his cologne beneath the tang of petrol.

Suddenly one of the other instructors opened the door next to Jess. The wind intensified along with her heart rate. Her stomach hollowed out as she saw the patchwork of Salisbury below her. Not Paris at all.

Why am I doing thiiiiiissss?

A red light near the door pinged green.

'Okay!' said Kjell. 'That's us!'

'What? We're first?!' she panicked. Her stomach turned and her breakfast of scrambled eggs and bacon threatened to re-appear. What if she vomited while she was in the air? She'd never be able to show the video to anyone.

'Yup! Lucky us!' he shouted near her ear. 'Trust me, it's better than sitting around and waiting.'

Her poor heart. Today it rode a rollercoaster of fear as it pumped even harder. The photographer climbed out of the plane and clung to some bars outside, like he was stepping out for a leisurely breath of fresh air.

Kjell scooted them towards the door, so her legs dangled outside over the void. All she wanted to do was scoot them back in the other direction, into the safety of the plane, but she was no longer in charge. Kjell was the boss. This jump would be happening, ready or not. She tried not to look down.

She looked down.

Shiiiiiiiiiiittttt.

Seconds stretched as they lingered on the edge.

The photographer jumped first. A moment later, Kjell followed.

Jess was flying!

All the fear that had been crashing through her moments ago disintegrated as the wind flattened the front of her jumpsuit to her body. *Free falling*, she realised, didn't really describe the sensation because she didn't feel like she was falling at all. The air acted like a huge pillow, cushioning her. Kjell tapped her shoulder to remind her to cactus her arms, which she dutifully did.

This was amazing.

The roar of the wind thundered in her ears. A loud whoop started in the pit of her belly and travelled up her body and out through her mouth. 'I did it!' she screamed. Kjell spun her around in circles. Out of the corner of her eye, she detected the no-fear cameraman diving and somersaulting around them to get the best angles of her fall. Show off.

In the distance, she clocked Stonehenge, standing strong for thousands of years.

That deep sensation of peace she had been chasing came over her again, reminiscent of the helicopter ride. She loved this. Heck, she was going to train as a skydiver. She wanted this feeling all the time.

From 15,000 feet, the website said the free fall would last about a minute. Jess had developed a system for categorising minutes. A planking minute—that is, the length of time that passed while one is holding a plank position—always seemed to last forever, whereas a reading-a-good-book minute always flew by too fast. Unfortunately, this minute fell into the latter category and, before she knew it, the parachute opened up, pulling them backwards. The engine-sound of the air transformed into silence. They floated gently, weightless as feathers, and she thought about a book she read to her kids about Albert Einstein, and how he came to link motion with gravity. She was experiencing science!

Kjell let her take control of the parachute ropes for a moment, which thrilled her. Being in charge even for just a few seconds gave her a powerful feeling in her gut. She had done this! What next?

Below, she saw her photographer about to land and watched him avidly, taking mental notes. His feet touched down, he ran a few steps, and came to a stop. Then he deftly detached from his parachute.

The ground was rushing towards her now. No time to think. She lifted her legs into a tuck as instructed and waited for Kjell's feet to make contact with the earth. As soon it happened, she dropped her feet to the ground, running her legs. The sudden pull of gravity on her body made her feel temporarily heavy.

The euphoria was instantaneous.

She yelled, 'I want to go up again!' and danced around, hugging members of the ground team. What a buzz! Two months ago, she never would have considered doing something like this, but look at her now.

This felt right. This felt like who she was meant to be.

EXITING THE HANGAR, Jess headed back to her car, still grinning from ear-to-ear. The roar of another plane taking off with another load of expectant passengers ripped through the air. If they'd had space, she would have gone up again, but at £300 a pop, that could get expensive, fast. She was serious about getting qualified. This experience had definitely given her the bug.

She wound her way through the jammed parking lot. Closer to her car, she noticed something propped on her front windshield.

As she approached, Pierre, her broken piggy cookie jar from Paris, materialised. Golden lines crisscrossed his body, repairing the breaks where he had cracked.

Gabriel?

She spun around and searched for him. Another jolt of adrenaline shot through her body, and her breath hitched. She thought her heart had been beating fast before the jump; now, it hammered as though driven by a machine.

Holding her hand above her eyes, she studied the people in the nearby queue, checking in for their jump. Nope. No salt-n-pepper heads. She couldn't see him anywhere. Where was he?

Swinging around in the other direction, she saw him step out from behind a black van, a big self-satisfied grin on his face. '*Bonjour*, Jess.'

Her stomach fluttered. His deep, amused voice was the sweetest sound she'd ever heard.

'What the hell?' she gasped and ran up to him.

Don't get excited, she warned herself. He's probably just here on business. She shouldn't jump to any conclusions, even though delicious expectation and need surged through her. Awash with confusion and hope, she acted automatically and thwapped him on the chest.

'Ow!' he said, rubbing the spot over his heart.

'How did you know I was here?' she asked.

199

'My meddling sister, of course.'

Elodie. She had told him after seeing it on Jess's Facebook page. And then there was that donation…

Had he been here the whole time? Had he watched her jump? Had he—

Wait a second. A thought took hold, but surely it couldn't be true. She recalled smelling his cologne when she was in the plane…

'Were you my photographer?!'

'Guilty as charged. The most overqualified skydiving photographer in the world, at your service, ma'am.' He pretended to doff an imaginary cap.

She had so much adrenaline coursing through her system that only one reaction seemed right: she grabbed him and kissed him. His arms wound tight around her. She remembered the way their bodies fit together so perfectly like it had only been minutes since they last held each other.

Jess thought her heart had already taken a beating today, but it had more work to do. It knocked, feeling like it might burst out of her at any second. She hadn't realised how much she missed everything about him, from his scent to the feel of his lips to the slide of his tongue against hers. They kissed like they never wanted it to end.

He pulled back slightly. 'You were amazing up there,' he said, with an extra squeeze for emphasis. 'I was so proud.'

'How did you even manage…?'

'Turns out being a Magnum photographer still has some currency.' And there was that slow smile she loved so much. 'Plus one of the people in the office knew of my work. Plus I'm already a qualified skydiver.'

She threw her head back and laughed. She remembered him saying that in the helicopter, but thought he'd just said it to make her feel better. 'Of course you are. Any other secrets you want to share?' she asked with a crooked smile.

His eyes turned dark and solemn. 'I love you.'

Her breath caught. She swallowed, hard. 'Sorry, could you repeat that?'

'I love you, Jessica Smith.' Gabriel took a step back from her and gripped her by the shoulders. In the distance she heard a plane landing. 'I'm sorry it took me so long to find my way back to you. But I had work to do. I'm in therapy again…and I joined a support group for people who've lost their limbs in violent situations.'

Nodding, she said, 'I'm really proud of you. I know that couldn't have been easy.'

He glanced away. 'It wasn't…at first…but I've made new friends and found a way to be supportive to others who need help. And guess what?' He smiled. 'I also started a running club for amputees. We inspire our way around Paris every Sunday morning.'

Jess laughed again, still incredulous that he was here, declaring his love for her. Could this day get any better? Maybe she should buy a lottery ticket.

She closed the small gap between them and placed her hands on his chest. A familiar heat rushed through her at contact. 'And just in case you didn't realise, I love you, too.'

They kissed again with even more desperation, and she wondered how quickly they could get back to London.

Softening the kiss, he rested his forehead against hers, his expression turning serious for a second. 'I can't promise that it'll be easy, but I want to make room in my life for you. I'm here for two weeks with work. After that, we'll figure it out.'

'I like the sound of that.' Then she cleared her throat and said: '*Mon cousin de La Rochelle garde toujours une pelle dans son coffre.*'

Gabriel raised his non-scarred eyebrow, amused. 'You're learning French?'

'*Oui!*'

Chuckling, he said, 'Thank god. Your French was terrible.' He kissed her briefly on the lips before furrowing his brow. 'Although I'm not sure why anyone would need to know where your cousin from LaRochelle keeps his shovel.'

'Well, behave yourself and you won't find out.' Jess bit her lip.

'Yes, ma'am.'

EPILOGUE

THREE YEARS LATER

Too soon, the sound of the porter knocking on the tent woke Jess up. It was 11PM and they'd only managed a few hours' sleep. But this mountain wasn't going to climb itself.

'How are you feeling?' Jess asked Gabriel, who was snuggled in his sleeping bag next to her. After so many years together, she still couldn't believe that she had the pleasure of waking up next to this handsome man, even with his hair mussed, his jaw covered in five days' worth of stubble, and morning breath.

'Exhausted? You?' Groggily, he pushed himself up onto his elbows and leaned towards her for a quick kiss.

'Same. But I'm still glad we're here.'

He sat himself up and extricated his right leg from the sleeping bag. Wordlessly, she began massaging his stump for him. A daily ritual.

They disagreed about who came up with the idea of climbing Mount Kilimanjaro for charity. Gabriel insisted that she said it after they finished running the Paris Marathon. She claimed that it was Gabriel after he'd watched a documentary about some celebrities making the ascent. She remembered quite clearly: 'If they can do it, we can do it,' he'd said. Regardless, one of them had the bright idea. And here they were.

It was not easy.

In fact, it was hands-down the hardest thing she'd ever done. For five days, they'd been walking slowly, slowly up the trail with twelve other trekkers. The terrain ranged from scrubby grassland to moon-like stretches of brown, barren dirt. Sometimes the rise was so mild that she barely noticed they were going up. Other times, it grew steep and rocky. She lived in constant fear that Gabriel might take a wrong step, or a rock might roll under his prosthesis, but so far, he'd managed it. She continually fed him snacks along the way because amputees needed 30% more calories than non-amputees just to walk.

The headaches and nausea from the altitude surprised her early on the second day. Jess had expected them to appear much later in the trip. Thankfully, they had pills to mitigate these side effects.

A crew of sixty porters helped to carry their bags, cook their meals, and set up their tents. Jess was grateful for every single one of them and would be tipping them generously. They tripped up the mountain like it was nothing to them, but she had to admit it had been a struggle for her, even though both she and Gabriel were in good shape.

So far, they'd managed to raise £200,000 for the prosthetics charity they supported. Back in Paris, Jess had organised a huge, glittering gala where some generous friends had donated amazing money-can't-buy prizes. Gabriel also auctioned off a few pieces of his aerial artwork, and a seat next to him on his upcoming helicopter ride over Paris. Jess had already been up with him many, many times all over the world. It never got old. Nowadays, she even kept her eyes open the whole time.

The biggest prize of the night had been a week's holiday at their refurbished chateau. They'd finished it last year. When she first moved to Paris the summer after her skydive, she'd worked as a supply teacher at the American School with Elodie for a while, but then decided to retrain as an interior designer. Although she missed teaching sometimes, she had found her calling, and the results of her work at the chateau were featured in a famous French architectural magazine.

Jess was living her best life.

Most weekends, they'd head down there, along with Elodie, her wife and their young baby. Sometimes Fatima's wife and daughter came, too. They were practically members of the family. Johnson popped in, as well, with his Singaporean influencer wife, Yvonne, in tow. Jess could see why Yvonne had so many Instagram followers. The woman's muscles had muscles. She led a private Pilates class for the chateau guests that left them sore for days.

It was all good preparation for this trek. Now, Jess and Gabriel had to do the work of earning all those donations.

Although he hadn't complained once, the climb had been especially difficult for Gabriel with his prosthesis. They were putting in long hours and sometimes the silty terrain could be slippery, but he had powered through. Now they were about to attack the final ascent: a 7-hour climb on coarse dust, in the dark. On top of that it was windy and cold.

After a breakfast of watery porridge, the group lined up, ready to get started. Before they set off, one of the other trekkers, a popular DJ from a London radio station, clapped Gabriel on the back. 'You're such an inspiration, man.'

'Thanks, man,' said Gabriel graciously, before sharing an amused look with Jess. She pursed her lips to stop from laughing.

'Pole! Pole!' yelled their guide and they were off.

'FUCK ME, WHO SUGGESTED THIS AGAIN?' Gabriel huffed as they battled their way through an unexpected snowstorm after cresting Gilman Point.

'It was definitely you,' said Jess, her voice muffled by her scarf.

'Hmph,' he answered.

They were almost at the end. Only another half hour's walk. This was supposed to be the easy part now.

Two of their team hadn't made it, the high altitude and lack of oxygen forcing them to descend early, but the rest of the group struggled on towards Uhuru Peak.

The snowstorm died down almost as fast as it had started. Magically, the clouds disintegrated and the empty cerulean sky stretched overhead. It was only 6AM.

'I think I can see it.' Jess pointed. Not far in front of them, the wooden boards that proclaimed *Congratulations! You are now at Uhuru Peak Tanzania* slid into view.

They scrambled over the final metres.

'We made it!' yelled Jess, jumping up and down like she hadn't just been hiking for five days. She pulled down her scarf and kissed Gabriel in triumph. He wrapped his arms around her and, relieved at their arrival, they just hugged.

'Group photo!' shouted one of their fellow trekkers. They all gathered under the timber sign and grinned like the bunch of lunatics they were.

'Say *Tunaweza!*' called out the guide taking their photo.

'*Tunaweza!*' they chimed together. It meant '*we can*' in Swahili.

Jess breathed deeply and took in the amazing view. The sun had now fully risen, and the sky was a deep blue, the kind that hinted that there was a vast, black and endless expanse above it. The lunar landscape around her disappeared in the distance under thick snow, which led to a tall, white glacier. Beyond that, the earth below her was blanketed by a gossamer cloud cover, shielding the planet from her eyes. This had to be the most breathtaking sight she'd ever seen.

She had earned this view. She thought about the person she used to be before she met Gabriel: a woman afraid of risk, hankering after a 'normal' life. That night when Krish broke up with her had felt like the end of something, but really, it was the beginning. That moment had been a crossroads, and the path she took had led her here, 19,340 feet on top of the world with the man she loved—a man who taught her what it was to tackle life with both joy and ferocity every day.

Behind her, Gabriel cleared his throat. She turned around.

'Oh my god!' Jess exclaimed.

Gabriel was down on one knee, holding a small, blue velvet box out in front of him. She marvelled that he'd been carrying that up the mountain for five days.

Tears trickled down her face, freezing before they reached her jaw.

His voice shaky, Gabriel said, 'I have loved you since I first saw you drunk in a bar, crying over some other loser that broke your heart. Well, his loss was my gain because you are the most amazing, kind, brave, talented, caring woman I know. You are more important than oxygen to me. You push me to live to my fullest potential and— despite having a lot of it—you never take my bullshit. More than that, you save me on a daily basis. There is no one else in the world I'd rather spend the rest of my life with. Jessica Smith, will you marry me?'

Reader, she said yes.

THE END

Thank you for reading!
If you're not quite ready to let Gabriel
and Jess go, get another glimpse of their happily ever after in an
exclusive bonus epilogue.
Go juliaboggio.com/cs-bf
to get the download link.

And don't forget to look out for the next book in the
Photographers Trilogy, *Exposure!*—
available to pre-order now.

ACKNOWLEDGMENTS

Where do I even start? There are so many people I need to thank. First and foremost is my friend, Damian McGillicuddy, who kept asking me when I was going to put an amputee like him in one of my books. Representation matters! When I started thinking about Jess's story, I realised it was the perfect opportunity, and Gabriel was born. Damian, thank you for your honest chats with me and huge respect to your 'oxygen', Lesley, who 'saves you on a daily basis'.

Next, I have to thank Farrah Riaz for asking what happened to Jess after she beta-read *Chasing the Light*. If she hadn't asked the question, I might not have thought to write this story. And I'm so glad she did because I loved creating these characters and getting to know Jess better. All the unicorn stickers for you, Farrah!

I'm lucky that I happen to know a lot of talented photographers, so when I decided that Gabriel was an aerial photographer, I knew exactly who to call. Thank you to Tony Hewitt for the technical and mental insight into what you do so beautifully. The *Toy Story* clouds were for you. Check out Tony's amazing work at tonyhewitt.com. I also found Paris-specific details from *Paris from the Air* by Jeffrey Milstein.

As always, I have the most giving, talented group of beta readers. There's a little bit of you guys in everything I write: Jayne Rice, Juno

Goldstone, Farrah Riaz, and Joanna Lyons. Jess Popplewell and Amanda Scotland, thank you for cheering me on. The Coven rocks!

Merci beaucoup to Anais Hamelin and Whitney Cubbison for checking my French and the location details.

Bailey, you pulled another great cover out of the bag. Thanks for being on my team!

And as ever, I am eternally grateful to my family for putting up with mummy and her imaginary friends.

RECOMMENDED READING

If you are interested in true stories of war photographers, these are the books I recommend and that I read for writing *Camera Shy*:

- *Blood and Champagne: The Life & Times of Robert Capa* by Alex Kershaw
- *Unreasonable Behaviour: An Autobiography* by Don McCullin
- *Shutterbabe: Adventures in Love & War* by Deborah Copaken Kogan
- *Here I Am: The Story of Tim Hetherington, War Photographer* by Alan Huffman
- *It's What I Do: A Photographer's Life of Love & War* by Lynsey Addario

If you enjoyed
* *CAMERA*SHY* *
* * *
please review it on
Goodreads and Amazon!
Every review helps a
new reader find my books

♡ Julia

P.S. Did you find
the Dirty Dancing
reference? ☺

OUT NOW!

Shooters

When Stella Price's life explodes, she needs to reinvent herself, fast. So she picks up her old camera and decides to try her hand at wedding photography. Easy, right?

Wrong. It's competitive and hard. If she doesn't find help soon, she's going to fail at this, too.
Then she meets Connor Knight, the best wedding photographer in the world. He's talented, arrogant, ridiculously hot, and people claim he's a brilliant mentor. She dislikes him almost immediately.

But he notices her talent and offers to teach her —probably more than she wants to learn.

Their clashes lead to an unexpected whirlwind of passion, but Stella struggles to frame a future with a man who distrusts "happily ever afters". Can Stella learn from her past mistakes and teach Connor about real love before he disappears from the picture?

AVAILABLE FROM AMAZON

OUT NOW!

Chasing the Light

On the outside, Francesca March is a confident woman
and an entrepreneur, but on the inside,
she's a quivering mess with a painful secret.

When she runs into ex-boyfriend Krish Kapadia,
old feelings bubble to the surface,
but her instincts tell her to push him away again.

He's still sexy. He still has a bad habit of rescuing her.
But she's still broken. Plus he's got a nice new girlfriend
who could easily win a beauty contest. His life is working
out just how he's always wanted.

But when Krish finally discovers her secret,
will that change his plans? Or will he stay the course
with the life he always said he wanted?
And even if he did choose her, would Francesca let him?

AVAILABLE FROM AMAZON

ABOUT THE AUTHOR

Photo by Giles Christopher

Originally from New Jersey, Julia moved to London in her early twenties. She worked as an advertising copywriter until discovering her love of photography on a 6-month trip around South America. She started a wedding photography business which received some great PR when her own *Dirty Dancing*-themed wedding dance went viral on YouTube. She appeared on *Richard & Judy* and *The Oprah Winfrey Show*, where she danced with Patrick Swayze. In 2009 she opened a luxury portrait studio and has photographed everyone from the Queen to Queen, the band. After 15 years as a photographer, she returned to her first love: writing. Julia lives in Wimbledon with her Welsh husband, two children, and an oddly possessive cat.

facebook.com/juliaboggio

instagram.com/juliaboggio

tiktok.com/@juliaboggiowriter

Swedish Photographer Martina Wärenfeldt reading Shooters

Australian Photographer Kelly Brown reading Shooters

UK Photographer Damian McGillicuddy reading Shooters

US Photographer Melody Smith reading Shooters

US Photographer Justine Ungaro reading Chasing the Light

UK Photographer Tianna Jarrett-Williams reading Chasing the Light

Polish Photographer Maggie Robinson reading Chasing the Light

US Photographer Kristi Elias reading Chasing the Light

Milton Keynes UK
Ingram Content Group UK Ltd.
UKHW040837100124
435728UK00005B/213